*He was definitely the best looking guy she had ever been out with. She had an impossible urge to lean over and kiss him. Would that shock him? Was it worth a try? She knew, of course, she would never have the nerve to do it. Could a guy as smart and as good looking as Tom Stearns really be interested in Becky Johnson? Maybe. She sighed. With a start, she realized that Tom had stopped talking. He was staring at her with a half smile on his face.*

Dear Readers:

Thank you for your many enthusiastic and helpful letters. In the months ahead we will be responding to your suggestions. Just as you have requested, we will be giving you more First Loves from the boy's point of view; and for you younger teens, younger characters. We will be featuring more contemporary, stronger heroines, and will be publishing, again in response to your wishes, more stories with bittersweet endings. Since most of you wanted to know more about our authors, from now on we will be including a short author's biography in the front of every First Love.

For our Book Club members we are publishing a monthly newsletter to keep you abreast of First Love plans and to share inside information about our authors and titles. These are just a few of the exciting ideas that First Love from Silhouette has in store for you.

Nancy Jackson
Senior Editor
Silhouette Books

# RESEARCH FOR ROMANCE
## Erin Phillips

*First Love from Silhouette*
Published by Silhouette Books New York
**America's Publisher of Contemporary Romance**

SILHOUETTE BOOKS, a Division of Simon & Schuster, Inc.
1230 Avenue of the Americas, New York, N.Y. 10020

ISBN: 0-671-53396-7

First Silhouette Books printing May, 1984

10 9 8 7 6 5 4 3 2 1

America's Publisher of Contemporary Romance

Printed in the U.S.A.

# 1

Aphids!" the red-faced woman sputtered. "All over my begonias."

Becky Johnson, standing behind the desk of the River Bend Public Library, did not know what aphids were. But she thought maybe the woman needed some books on gardening.

"We have a whole section on gardening," Becky said as she walked around the desk.

"I'm going to get them this time," the woman said menacingly. "Once and for all."

Becky led the woman to the proper section and helped her find several books on insects and begonias. The woman settled down at a table and, still muttering to herself, began to pore over one of the books.

Becky loved books and loved to read and had been thrilled when she got her part-time job at the library. Even though she had been coming there ever since she was seven years old—the very first book she had checked out was *Green Eggs and Ham* by Dr. Seuss—she was nervous when she first started at the beginning of June. But now, almost a month later, she knew most of the library procedures and was very good at helping people find the books and the information that they needed, even information on aphids! Becky went back to her position behind the front desk. The library was never very busy on Saturday afternoons.

It was a beautiful, sunny day and her two best friends, L.W. and Laurie K., had gone to the local swimming pool. She leaned her elbows on the counter top and pictured all the kids at the pool. Jeff, Laurie K.'s new flame, would be doing silly dives off the high board, trying to show off for her. Laurie K. would be pretending that he was really dumb but she would be secretly enjoying it. L.W., who was fair and red-headed, would have spent her usual twenty minutes in the sun, and would be reading a magazine under the shade of an umbrella. The other kids would be lying in the sun and listening to music. Becky wished that she could have joined them.

The one problem with working at the library was that the only males who ventured through the doors were either over sixty or under ten years old. Becky certainly hadn't expected to meet a lot of new boys at the library but it would be nice if someone her own age came in once in a while. Becky had a fantasy that one day some great looking, intelligent guy would come into the library and fall madly in love with her. He would be looking for books on literature or maybe some books on modern architecture. (She had read *The*

*Fountainhead* by Ayn Rand last summer and had been hooked on architects ever since.) After Becky had helped him find his books, he would say, "You're so smart . . . and so beautiful." Becky would blush demurely and he would say, "Come to Paris with me . . ."

Old Mr. Jones, who was asleep behind a copy of *The Wall Street Journal* in the Periodicals department, snorted and almost fell out of his chair. He woke up, rustled his paper importantly and glanced at Becky. She smiled at him. He nodded his head and went back to his newspaper. Mr. Jones was one of the regulars at the library. He came in everyday to read the paper and everyday he fell asleep.

Mrs. Francis, the head librarian, had told Becky about him. He was a retired lawyer who now dabbled in the stock market. He was a charming old gentleman, with courtly manners, who always dressed in a suit and a bow tie. He also donated generously to the library's acquisition fund. Mrs. Francis reasoned that he could doze just as much as he wanted to.

Becky glanced quickly around the room. Mrs. Francis was out to lunch and Miss Stevenson, a retired teacher who also worked part-time, was back in the office going over book orders. Becky decided that she would finish reading the latest copy of *Library Journal*, the trade magazine for librarians. She sat down behind the desk and turned to the section of reviews. Soon, she was absorbed in the reviews and the recommendations for the forthcoming books.

"Excuse me," a male voice said.

Becky looked up from the magazine. She almost did a double take. One of the best looking guys she had ever seen was standing on the other side of the counter. He had dark, curly brown hair, a wide forehead and smoky blue eyes. He was smiling at her.

Becky stood up quickly. "Yes?"

"I wonder if you could tell me where the biography section is?"

Becky had never seen him before. She knew just about everybody at River Bend High, especially the juniors and seniors since she was going to be a junior next fall.

"I'm looking for a biography of Albert Einstein," he said, "and I wondered if it would be in the biography section or the science section?"

"Probably in the biography section," she said. "I'll show you." She started to come around the corner of the counter.

"I can find it," he said. "Just point me in the right direction."

"That's all right," Becky said, smiling. "Follow me." She started for the corner of the room where the biographies and the autobiographies were shelved. Suddenly, she was glad that she had worn her new yellow blouse and her new white slacks today. The yellow blouse accented her light brown, shoulder length hair and highlighted her dark green eyes.

She stopped in front of a shelf of books and pointed to the titles on Einstein.

"Was there a particular book that you were looking for?"

"Not really," he said. "I'm taking a History of Science course at Abercrombie and I thought I'd just do some background reading."

Becky's heart sank. Abercrombie College was a small, private college a few miles from town.

That meant that he was already in college. He wouldn't be even remotely interested in a high school junior. "Have you tried the Abercrombie library?" she asked.

He had pulled down a book from the shelf and was looking at the table of contents. "What? Oh. Yes I have. But I was just riding by and I thought I'd stop in. This one looks pretty good. Have you read it?"

Becky shook her head.

He opened the book to the beginning of a chapter and began to skim the page. Becky looked at him closely. He was several inches taller than she—probably about six feet tall. He was tanned and his hair was bleached a warm coppery color on the top and around his sideburns. He was slim and was dressed in a blue and white striped rugby shirt and cut-off jeans. A bright blue backpack was slung over one shoulder. She leaned a little closer to him. He smelled fresh and outdoorsy. Sort of like green leaves and sunshine.

"Could you show me where the science section is?" he asked, looking up from the book.

Becky blushed. Had he noticed her looking at him? "Sure," she said, trying to sound casual.

She took several steps, turned the corner and pointed out a double row of facing shelves. "Maybe I can help?" she said.

"Thanks," he said, "but I think I'll just browse around a little."

"Well, if you need any help . . ." She turned to go back to the desk.

"Oh wow," he exclaimed.

Becky turned around quickly.

"You've got *The Physicists*. I was looking for this. It's a history of famous physicists and the stories of their discoveries and . . ." He looked at her. "You must think I'm pretty weird, right? Einstein and physics and . . ."

Becky smiled and shook her head. "Not at all. We get some pretty strange people in here." She realized what she had just said. She blushed to the roots of her hair. Me and my big mouth she thought. "I'm sorry," she stammered. "I meant . . . I didn't mean . . . I . . ."

"That's O.K.," he said, smiling. "I know what you meant."

Becky breathed a sigh of relief.

"I'm Tom Stearns," he said.

"Becky Johnson."

Neither one of them seemed to know what to say next. Becky heard some voices behind her. A woman and a little boy were standing by the front desk.

"I better get back to work," she said quickly.

"It's nice to meet you," he said.

Becky turned and headed for the desk. Tom Stearns. She repeated his name to herself. What a nice name. Tom Stearns. Wasn't it wonderful that she hadn't gone to the pool with L.W. and Laurie K.? Wasn't it wonderful that she had gotten her job at the library? She smiled at the aphids lady who was still mumbling to herself, her nose buried in a book. She smiled at the sounds of Mr. Jones's light snoring coming from behind his newspaper. She gave the woman and her little boy a dazzling smile and asked if she could help them.

"I wonder if you have any books on rockets?" the woman asked. "Sean is just crazy about rockets."

"Hello, Sean," Becky said. He was about seven

or eight years old. "We've got lots of books on rockets."

In the picture book section of the Children's department, Becky pulled out several books for the little boy. "Here's one on the history of flight," she said. "It should have quite a bit on rockets." She handed the book to him. "And here's one on NASA—you know, where they shoot the rockets into space. And here," she said, pausing dramatically and holding up a brand-new book, "is one on the space shuttle."

Sean's eyes had gotten big and he was looking excitedly at the book on the shuttle.

"Why don't we take the books over to the table," Becky suggested, "and you can sit down and then decide which ones you want to check out." She helped him and his mother get settled.

"Thanks so much," the mother said.

Becky ruffled Sean's curly blond hair. He was already lost in the book on the space shuttle.

Becky loved the excitement and the wonder that came into children's eyes when she was able to provide them with a book that caught their fancy. She really enjoyed introducing them to some of the special magic that only a book could provide.

She was still thinking about Sean and his rockets when she reached the front desk. How could she have forgotten about Tom Stearns? She looked around for him. He was still in the science section. He had dropped his backpack on the floor and was leaning up against one of the shelves. His back was to her and he was completely absorbed in a book. Even across the room, his hair had a bright, shiny gleam to it. His shoulders

11

were broad and completely filled out his tight, knit shirt. His waist was narrow and his long legs tapered gracefully down to his shoes. A definite fox.

He was intelligent, too, she decided. Physics and science were pretty serious subjects. She couldn't tell whether he was one of those boy geniuses or not.

Intelligence was one of Becky's strong points. Well, sometimes it was one of her strong points. She did well in school and was ranked fourth in her class. She remembered what L.W. had once said. "Becky," L.W. had begun, using the voice she always used when she was about to make a pronouncement, "you act too intelligent. It scares the boys off."

"But what about you?" Becky had asked in amazement. L.W. was ranked second in the class.

"I don't count," L.W. had said. "Everybody knows that I aspire to the halls of higher learning and they just accept me for that. But you always talk about books and literature . . . and it scares people off."

Becky had puzzled over that one for a long time. Then she had decided that if she had to act dumb in order to attract boys, they probably weren't worth attracting in the first place.

Becky glanced at the clock. It was ten minutes to two. Mrs. Francis would be back from lunch at two and then she would have to go. She hoped she would get to talk to Tom before she had to leave.

Sean and his mother approached the desk.

"Did you decide on some books?" Becky asked. Sean nodded his head and slid the books he was carrying up on the counter. Becky took the mother's library card and checked the books out. Sean clutched the books tightly when she handed them back to him.

"Thanks again," the mother said. "We'll probably be back next week for some more."

Becky watched them as they went out through the glass doors of the library. Near the entrance, a large Irish Setter came into view. He was wagging his tail and trying to lick Sean on the face. Sean stopped and patted him gingerly, slightly afraid, the way that little kids are always afraid of large dogs.

"I see Maxwell's made a friend." Becky whirled around. It was Tom. That was the second time today that he had surprised her. He was smiling and watching the little boy and the dog.

"Is he yours?"

"Yeah," Tom said. "He loves kids."

"He's really pretty."

"Thanks."

They both watched as the little boy and his mother moved off to their car. Maxwell, the dog, lay down in the middle of the sidewalk, right in front of the doors.

Becky looked back at Tom. He was carrying three thick, serious-looking books. He set them on the counter in front of her. "These should keep me busy," he said.

Becky asked for his library card. For a second he looked surprised. Then he began to look embarrassed.

"Sorry," he said, "I don't have a library card. I hadn't even thought about that." He looked at her for help.

"That's no problem," Becky said. "I can give you a temporary card today and you can fill out the application and pick up your new card next week."

"Thanks," he said.

"Now," Becky said, pulling out an application, "are you a resident of River Bend?"

Tom said yes.

"Are you eighteen years old?" She hoped she didn't sound too official.

"I'm seventeen."

Becky's heart gave a little leap in her chest. He wasn't a college student after all. Unless, and her heart sank at the prospect, he *was* one of those boy geniuses or something. Although a boy genius might be interesting . . .

"Unless you're eighteen," she said, "you have to get your parent's signature on the card." She paused. "It's just the rules, you know."

Tom ran his hand through the side of his hair. "We just moved here. I used to use the library a lot in Boston and I just assumed that I had a card . . ."

Becky wasn't supposed to carry on extended conversations but since the library was almost empty she decided to bend the rules a little and talk to him.

He told her that they had just moved to River Bend from Boston. His father was the new president of Abercrombie College. That's the reason he got to take a course there. He would be a senior in high school in the fall. Becky was a good listener and that encouraged Tom to talk. He told her about Boston, how weird it was to move to a new town in the Midwest, and talked a little about the college.

As she listened to him, Becky realized that Tom didn't have any of the self-consciousness that so many of the boys his age had. He talked evenly, forming his sentences carefully and looked directly at her. His voice was warm and deep. The low whispers that they were conversing in—after all, it was the library—seemed to wrap them in a special world all their own.

Becky decided that he had probably spent a lot of time around adults, especially if his father had been associated with colleges, and he had learned how to carry on a conversation and how to be relaxed around people.

Becky tried not to look at the clock but she was expecting Mrs. Francis to come back any minute.

"I better be going," he said. "You've got work to do."

"It's just that I'm not supposed to stand around and talk," she said, smiling. "But why don't I hold these books for you until Monday and you can get the application signed and pick them up next week."

"That would be great," he said.

"It's no trouble at all. I'll just put your name on them and put them over here on the Reserved shelf." She got a piece of paper and a pen and asked him to spell his name for her.

"S-t-e-a-r-n-s," he spelled slowly.

She was dying to find out where he lived and where he was going to go to high school and everything else she could about him but she tried to act cool and professional.

She put a rubber band around the books, slipped the name tag under the band and put the books behind the counter.

"Thanks a lot," Tom said. He paused and looked at her as if he wanted to say something else.

Becky held her breath.

"It's Becky, right? Becky Johnson?"

She nodded her head. Hoping that he would say something like, "Would you like to have a Coke when you get off work?" Or, even better, "You are so smart . . . and so beautiful. Come to Paris with me."

Instead, he ran his hand through the side of his hair again. "Well, I guess I'll see you Monday."

Becky let out her breath slowly. "I'll be here," she said, trying to make her voice sound casual, "in the afternoon."

He adjusted his backpack, said goodbye and walked toward the doors. Outside, the dog leaped up and began wagging his tail and dancing all over the sidewalk. Tom bent down and scratched his ears and said something to him before turning to wave to Becky through the glass.

She waved back, then Tom disappeared from sight for a moment and then reappeared riding an expensive-looking ten-speed bicycle. Maxwell was trotting along beside the rear wheel. Becky watched him as he rode the length of the plate glass windows and was totally out of sight.

Becky walked over to the Reserved shelf. Gently, she touched the piece of paper with his name on it.

## 2

**B**ecky was so excited about meeting Tom that she was about ready to burst by the time she got home. She dashed into her bedroom, dumped her purse along with the books she had checked out onto her bed and dragged the hall telephone into her room.

"Dinner's in half an hour," her father called from the kitchen.

"O.K." Becky yelled back.

Hurriedly, she shut the door to her bedroom, plopped down on her bed and dialed Laurie K.'s number. Laurie K. was the one she always talked to first about boys. Becky tapped her foot anxiously against the floor as the phone rang. First ring—his eyes are so blue. Second ring—he's so tall. Third ring—he's really smart. Fourth ring—he just moved here and he's going to be a senior. Fifth ring—why doesn't somebody answer? Sixth ring—maybe nobody's home. Seventh ring—just for good measure. Becky hung up the phone.

Excitedly, she dialed L.W.'s number. First ring —his eyes are so blue. Second ring—he's so . . .

"Hello," L.W.'s mother said.

Becky tried to keep her voice calm. "Could I speak to L.W?"

"Becky?"

"Hello, Mrs. Wilson," she said politely. "Is L.W. there?"

"She's in the shower," Mrs. Wilson said. "I'll tell her you called."

Becky thanked her and hung up the phone. Now, she really was going to burst. Who could she tell about Tom? Her younger brother, Todd, was in the family room watching reruns. Could she talk to him? No, she decided. Even though they'd been getting along better recently, she really couldn't confide in him. Her mother wasn't home from work yet. Her father? Should she just waltz into the kitchen and announce that she'd met the boy of her dreams in the library today? Becky could talk to both her parents and usually told them most of what was going on in her life. Since she had not dated very much there had never been a lot of boy-stuff to talk to them about. She didn't know if, when the time came to talk to them about her love life—if the time ever came—she would be able to confide in them.

She decided to call Laurie K.'s number again. After the sixth ring she put the receiver back on the hook. How dare Laurie K. be gone at this most critical moment? And how dare L.W. be in the shower? How could she be doing something as mundane as taking a *shower*, when Becky was about to explode every time she even thought about the way Tom had smiled at her, or the way he had turned around and waved to her?

Becky fell back on the bed, intent on day-dreaming about him for awhile. Unfortunately, one of the books that she had brought home jabbed her in the small of the back. Reluctantly, she got up off the bed, replaced the phone on its table in the hall and came back into her room. She picked up the three books and, tucking her legs underneath her, settled comfortably in the middle of the bed.

The first book was titled *How to Raise and Train Irish Setters*. The photograph of the dog on the cover looked just like Maxwell. The second book, almost new and covered with a protective plastic cover was *Boston: A History and a Guide*. The third book, the heaviest of all three, was *The Physicists*. As soon as Tom had left the library and Becky had come back down to earth, she had decided she better do a little research. Becky sincerely believed that you could find out just about anything you wanted from a book and, besides, it never hurt to do a little "background" reading.

Since the library was closed on Sunday, she didn't think it would hurt to borrow *The Physicists* and return it first thing on Monday. Then, when Tom came in to pick up his books, she could sort of casually mention that she had taken a look at the book. She hoped he would be impressed. It would also give them something to talk about. Since she didn't know much about him yet, she decided that Irish Setters and Boston were two other topics she should explore.

Becky heard the familiar sound of her mother's Volkswagen bug pull into the driveway. In a couple of minutes, her mother poked her head in Becky's doorway.

"Hi," she said. "Have a good day?"

"Hi, Mom," Becky said brightly. "I had a terrific day. How about you?"

"Busy," her mother answered. "The chef says dinner's in two minutes. Just as soon as I get out of these clothes." Her mother disappeared down the hallway.

Becky's mother was the assistant manager of a jewelry store at the shopping mall on the outskirts of town. She had gone back to work five years ago and seemed to enjoy it although Becky knew that it was partly because they also needed the extra money.

Becky stacked the three books—Tom's books, she decided to call them—on her bedside table and wandered toward the kitchen. Since her mother had to work on Saturdays, Becky's father always cooked dinner on Saturday nights. The aroma coming from the kitchen smelled delicious. Her father was a good cook and always did one of his specialties for dinner. Tonight it was spaghetti and meat sauce. She was famished.

The dining room table was already set when she entered the kitchen. Her father was stirring a giant pot of tomato sauce with a wooden spoon. He leaned down and kissed her on the forehead.

"Hungry?"

"Starved."

He smiled at her and turned off the flame under the sauce.

Becky sat down on one of the counter stools near the sink and watched her father as he pulled a steaming loaf of garlic bread from the oven.

Todd popped into the kitchen. "What's next?"

"Slice the bread and put it on the table," her father said, handing him the loaf.

Todd came over to the counter next to Becky. "So," he said, "how's Marion the Librarian?"

"Fine," Becky said sweetly. "How's Todd the Toad?"

Todd gave her a dirty look and started slicing the bread.

Becky sat right on her stool and did not offer to help. Her father's rule was that with two Saturday-working women in the house, the men took care of the meal. Becky loved the rule.

Todd carried the bread into the dining room. He had recently turned fourteen. He looked as though he'd grown an inch since breakfast. He was already as tall as their father, which was five-ten, and which he made a big deal about. The resemblance between father and son was remarkable, Becky thought, as she watched them bustle around the kitchen. They had exactly the same dark, curly brown hair and the same big brown eyes. Todd was going to be a very handsome man someday. But right now, he was lost somewhere between *Star Wars* and adulthood. He was all legs and feet and elbows. Becky alternately despised him, tolerated him and liked him. Most of the time it was a pain in the kazoo having a brother who was two years younger than she. It was only in the last few months that they had been able to come to an occasional truce and, when Todd was in one of his more mature moods, actually talk to each other.

Her father poured a giant bowl of meat sauce. "Becky," he called, "soup's on."

"Coming."

Her father heaped a platter with spaghetti while Todd carefully carried the sauce into the other room. He dashed back in and grabbed the platter of spaghetti.

"Salad, bread, spaghetti, meat sauce," her father counted. "Todd? Water?"

"It's on. It's on," he yelled.

"That's it," her father said. He bowed from the waist and offered his arm to Becky. "Shall we dine?"

Becky hopped off her stool, curtsied and took his arm. They promenaded into the dining room.

Her mother was already at the table. She looked hungry and a little tired.

While they ate, her mother talked about the jewelry store, her father talked about the car repairs and Todd talked about his upcoming Little League baseball game. Becky was dying to talk about Tom but kept silent. Her father asked about the library so she told them about the aphids lady and about Sean, the rocket boy.

Then she remembered something. "I wonder," she said, trying to sound as if she had just thought of it, "where my bicycle is?"

"Your bike!" Todd said. "I thought you said you wouldn't be caught dead riding a bicycle?"

Becky ignored him, although what he said was true. About three years ago, everybody had decided that bike riding was for kids and they all had, blithely putting their childhoods behind them, stopped pedaling around town.

"I was just thinking," she said, "that it might be sort of fun to ride it—once in a while." Becky had loved her shiny green ten-speed when she had gotten it for her tenth birthday but she couldn't remember the last time she had actually ridden it—or seen it.

"Isn't it in the garage?" her father said.

"No," her mother said, "I think it's in the basement. In the storage area."

"I don't believe it," Todd said, jumping back into the conversation, "Marion's going to ride her bicycle!"

"Look. Toad . . ."

The phone rang.

"I'll get it." Todd jumped up from the table and ran into the kitchen.

Becky's heart turned over. Could it be Tom? Could he be calling all the Johnsons in the telephone book, desperately searching for her?

"We're eating," she heard Todd say. "I'll give her the message."

One of the Johnsons' rules were no telephone conversations during dinner.

Todd came back into the room. "One of your dopey friends," he said to Becky, "L.W."

Becky raced through her spaghetti, ate the last leaf of her salad and asked to be excused. She flew to her room and dialed L.W.'s number.

L.W. picked up on the second ring. Becky erupted with her news of Tom. L.W. listened intently, asked the right questions and then, in her usual balloon-pricking manner said, "He sounds wonderful Becky, but . . ."

Becky grimaced and held the phone away from her ear. She had a pretty good idea what L.W. was going to say. When she put the phone back to her ear, L.W. was saying, ". . . he sounds incredible but you did just meet him. It's not like he asked you out or . . ."

"You're such a party pooper," Becky interrupted her. "He's gorgeous and we're going to fall totally in love. I know it."

L.W. changed the subject. "You should have seen Jeff at the pool today. He acted like he was Mr. America."

Becky smiled at L.W.'s description. Jeff was on the football and basketball teams and had a really good build. The only problem was that he was sort of dumb. Well, not really dumb, Becky decided, just sort of, well—dumb. But he was really cute. Not as good looking as Tom, she thought hastily, but he was a real hunk.

"The big news," L.W. said, "is that he didn't ask Laurie K. out tonight."

"How come?" Becky asked, suddenly interested.

"I haven't the faintest idea," L.W. said. "She's dying to know what's going on." L.W. paused for a few seconds. "So," she said, "it's 'We Three' once again, for the evening."

They decided they would maybe go to a movie, definitely cruise around town a little and spend the night at L.W.'s. They always stayed overnight at her house. Becky checked with her parents, while L.W. stayed on the line. L.W. said she would pick her up at seven-thirty.

As Becky took a shower, she thought about "We Three." She couldn't quite remember how they had become best friends. It just seemed to have happened when they were all in the sixth grade. The strange thing about it was having two best friends who were both named Laurie. (L.W.'s real name was Laurie Wilson and Laurie K. was really Laurie Kaynor.) It was particularly confusing on the telephone. Finally, Becky's father had started calling Laurie Wilson, Laurie W. Then the other girl had decided that she wanted an initial so she became Laurie K. Next, Laurie W. had shortened her nickname to L.W.—which suited her perfectly. And Laurie K. had stayed Laurie K., which also suited her better than just the name Laurie did. Throughout all the shortening of names and the use of initials, Becky had remained just plain Becky.

Becky dressed carefully and put on her usual dab of eye liner and lipstick. She doubted that they would run into Tom but she wanted to look her best just in case.

She was ready on the dot of seven-thirty and was waiting in the family room when she heard the familiar honk of L.W.'s horn. She said goodbye to her parents and dashed out the door. L.W. always drove since she had gotten a new, red Rabbit convertible for her sixteenth birthday. The top was down and Laurie K. was sitting in the passenger seat. Becky threw her overnight bag and her sleeping bag into the backseat and climbed into the car.

Before they were even out of the driveway, she had launched into her story of Tom for Laurie K. Laurie K. was, as Becky knew she would be, ecstatic at the news.

"I hate to interrupt this happy narrative," L.W. said, stopping the car at a red light, "but what are we going to do this evening?"

They couldn't decide on a movie. Of the two movies at the shopping center, one was a bad romantic comedy and the other was a serious drama. L.W. had researched the movies. They decided to just cruise around.

"Hey," Laurie K. said, "where does Tom live?"

Becky said she didn't know.

"We shall simply call directory assistance," L.W. said.

"They'll only give you the phone number," Becky said, suddenly not crazy about this new scheme.

"Just watch," L.W. said, and turned into the Kroger parking lot where there was a public telephone.

She parked the car, fumbled for a dime in her purse and before Becky could stop her, had dialed information.

Becky followed her to the phone.

"Oh, I hope you can help me," L.W. crooned into the phone. "I need a River Bend number. A new listing. Stearns. She spelled the name carefully. "You do have a listing! On St. Louis Street?" She raised her eyebrows at Becky. St. Louis Street was *the* classy street in town. "Now, I know you're not supposed to give out addresses but they just moved here and we're friends from out-of-town—from Boston—and we want to pop in and surprise them. Three two seven St. Louis Street. Thank you *so* much." She hung up the phone triumphantly.

They piled back into the car.

"St. Louis Street," Laurie K. said. "He's sounding better and better."

L.W. headed the car toward that part of town. Becky was having serious second thoughts about this particular adventure. Maybe, she thought desperately, she could just leap out of the car and wait for them here at the Burger Chef. L.W.

raced around the corner before Becky could say anything.

Curiosity, however, got the better of Becky and she decided she would crouch down in the backseat so no one could see her and just take a peek at his house. She did want to know everything about him.

They turned onto the proper street and L.W. slowed the car to a crawl as they tried to read the house numbers.

"It's the old Reynolds house," Laurie K. cried.

There it was. Three two seven. The old Reynolds house was a rambling, three-story Victorian. It was on a large corner lot and was surrounded by an antique cast-iron fence.

"Do you realize how much that house cost?" L.W. said. Her mother dabbled in local real estate.

"How much?" Becky and Laurie K. asked at the same time.

"Actually, I don't know how much it cost," she admitted, "but Mrs. Middleman at the real estate office thought she'd never sell it—it was so expensive."

"Drive by again," Laurie K. commanded.

L.W. turned the car around. Becky had completely forgotten to keep herself hidden in the back. "Drive by the side," she said.

L.W. turned into the side street. There was light in what looked like the dining room and a light in one of the second-floor bedrooms.

"There's his bicycle," Becky whispered excitedly. "By the garage."

"Bicycle!" both girls in the front seat exclaimed.

"Well, he's from Boston," Becky said. "They must have a lot of bicycles in Boston."

"It's a beautiful old house," Laurie K. said.

"That was certainly a thrill," L.W. said. "What shall we do next?"

"Let's drive by Jeff's," Becky suggested. One good turn deserved another, she thought.

"That's the best idea we've had all evening," Laurie K. said.

L.W. headed the car for the subdivision where Jeff lived. There were a few lights on in Jeff's house but his Trans-Am was not in the driveway.

"I wonder where he is?" Laurie K. said. "He didn't say anything to me about having to do something tonight."

"He's probably just out messing around," Becky said. "Maybe we'll run into him."

They did the circuit. They drove through the parking lot of MacDonald's, the parking lot of Dog n' Suds—although nobody really hung out there anymore, the parking lot of Taco Bell and cruised quickly by the Pancake House. There was no sign of Jeff so they drove by his house again. Still no Trans-Am.

Next, they checked out the other side of town. L.W. cruised through the parking lot of the Pizza Hut, zipped through the parking lot of Fish and Chips—*nobody* went to Fish and Chips, by Burger Chef and through the deserted lot of A & W.

"The town is dead. Dead," Laurie K. said. "Where is everybody?"

Becky had hoped to run into Tom. She had been watching all the cars carefully and hadn't seen anyone that even remotely resembled him. She wondered what he had done in Boston on

Saturday nights? And, more importantly, what he was doing tonight in River Bend?

L.W. turned around and headed for the shopping mall which was back on the other side of town. It was small and only had a few shops. The really big mall was in Alton, which was about fifteen miles away.

As they drove past the bowling alley, the K-Mart, the weed-littered empty lot along the road, Becky tried, for the first time, to evaluate River Bend, Illinois. She had never thought about it much before. It was just the nice, small town where she had been born and where she was growing up. But to Tom, coming from a beautiful city like Boston, did this little town of ten thousand people, in the middle of a corn field, look ugly and unreal? Did the things that Becky had always taken for granted like the discount gasoline stations, the new fast-food restaurants, even the fake wood-covered shopping mall, look cheap and small and constricting? Becky had never judged the town before; she had just accepted it . . .

"You're awfully quiet back there," Laurie K. said, turning around in the seat to peer at her. "Are you okay?"

"Sure," Becky said briefly. Should she mention her thoughts to them? No, she decided. Laurie K. would just think she was crazy. And L.W. would just dismiss the town for what it was to her—the place she was leaving as soon as she went away to college.

The parking lot at the cinema was almost empty. They had evidently made the right decision about going to the movies. They checked out the cars in the lot of the video arcade and didn't recognize any of them. They still had not seen Jeff.

"Let's go to the Dairy Bar," Laurie K. suggested.

L.W. spun the car around in front of Sam's Tropical Fish World and turned, once again, toward the other side of town. The Dairy Bar was a small ice cream and root beer stand that was only open in the summertime. When they pulled into the parking lot there were only two other cars there. One was filled with two women and three or four screaming kids. The other was occupied by an old couple, silently licking at ice cream cones.

"Was there a party we didn't know about?" L.W. asked.

"No," Laurie K. said, "I checked around this afternoon."

They decided that it was just an off night. Laurie K. went up to the counter to get them all Tabs and came back in a couple of minutes.

"Hey," she said, settling back into the front seat. "There's Jonathan."

A red Toyota had pulled into the lot.

"Hey, Jonathan," Laurie K. yelled.

He waved and got out of his car. "Hi," he said, and came over to lean on the passenger side of the convertible. "Hi, Becky."

They all said hello.

"What are you doing in town?" Laurie K. asked.

"I'm just home for the weekend."

Jonathan had gotten a job at a summer basketball camp for boys. It was held for eight weeks each summer on the campus of the University of

Illinois in Urbana. It had been a real coup for him to be selected as one of the assistant coaches.

"So, how's it going?" Laurie K. asked.

"I'm sort of assistant babysitter," he said, smiling. "The average age of the kids is twelve."

"But isn't it neat living in the dorm and everything?" Laurie K. asked.

"That's pretty cool," Jonathan said. He turned to Becky. "You'd really like the library," he said. "It's gigantic."

Becky smiled at him. She still felt uncomfortable around Jonathan Taylor. They had dated for a while last winter. Jonathan was the star of the junior varsity basketball team and even though he had only been a sophomore, had gotten to play in a few of the varsity games. Becky had read several books on basketball so she could understand the rules better and had gone to all of his games. She had liked Jonathan and enjoyed being with him. He was easygoing and had a good sense of humor. And even though he was really into basketball, he didn't act like a macho jock all the time. Unfortunately, Becky had developed a mad crush on a senior guy and she and Jonathan had drifted apart.

Becky remembered the first time Jonathan had kissed her. It was at a party at L.W.'s house after a game. They had been eating pepperoni pizza. When he kissed her in the kitchen, Becky had closed her eyes and tried to concentrate on the romantic moment, but all she could think about was pepperoni. After the kiss, he had hugged her close for a moment, which was nice, but she just couldn't get pepperoni out of her mind.

Laurie K. said that Jonathan was still carrying a torch for Becky. But she felt guilty and sort of embarrassed over the way she had gotten so silly over that senior guy and tried to avoid running into Jonathan whenever she could.

"Have you seen Jeff?" Laurie K. asked.

"I saw him this afternoon but I haven't seen him tonight."

Jeff and Jonathan were sort of buddies although Becky knew that he thought Jeff was a little too frivolous.

"Jeff's around somewhere," L.W. interposed, "admiring himself in a mirror, I'm sure."

Laurie K. turned and stuck out her tongue at L.W.

"So what are you guys up to?" he asked.

"The usual," L.W. said. "Looking for love—in all the wrong places."

"I know that song," Jonathan said, trying not to look at Becky.

"We better get going," Becky said.

"Yeah, me too," he said. He said goodbye and got back in his car.

L.W. started the car and they pulled out onto the road.

"Jonathan looks terrific," Laurie K. said. She scrunched around in the seat. "He's got it bad for you Becky."

Becky was silent.

"What happened between you two anyway?"

"You know what happened," Becky said. "Everett happened."

"Or, rather," L.W. said, turning onto Main Street, "Everett didn't happen."

"That was one of the dumbest crushes of your life," Laurie K. said.

Everett Barnes had been the president of the senior class and the star of the debating team. He was tall and had the most beautiful sad-looking, little-boy eyes that Becky had ever seen. She had been desperately in love with him all last spring.

"Did he ever speak to you?" L.W. asked.

Becky thought for a moment. "Twice," she said. "Once right after a Student Council assembly, and once in the hall of the main building."

Everett had never asked her out; had barely known that she was alive. "He seemed so mature," Becky said, "and so lonely."

"You were the one that was lonely—if you ask me," L.W. said.

But not anymore, Becky thought. At least, she hoped not anymore.

They drove by Jeff's one more time. The house was completely dark although the garage door was up and the space for his Trans-Am was empty.

"Another big night in the big city," L.W. said.

They all agreed that they might as well call it an evening.

## 3

**B**ecky changed clothes four times Monday morning. She didn't want to look too dressed up and she didn't want to look too casual and she just couldn't make up her mind. In desperation, she called Laurie K. at her parent's store and explained her problem.

"Wear that apple green blouse," Laurie K. commanded, "the one with the little ruffle at the neck. It makes your eyes look like Scarlet O'Hara's. And your white slacks. Simple."

"I had on my white slacks Saturday," Becky wailed.

There was a silence on the phone while Laurie K. pondered this new development. "Then your white skirt."

"You don't think it's too dressy?"

"Not at all."

"I don't know . . ."

"Do it, Becky," Laurie K. said imperiously. "If he doesn't ask you out, I personally will strip all the gears on his bicycle."

Becky thanked her and hung up the phone. She dressed carefully in the chosen outfit and surveyed herself in the full-length mirror on the closet door. She thought she looked pretty good.

She got to the library at eleven-thirty even though she wasn't supposed to be there until noon. She put her purse in the office and took up her post behind the counter. Tom's books were still on the Reserved shelf. She slipped the copy of *The Physicists* under the rubber band. Just to make doubly sure she hadn't missed him, she pulled out the new file cards and glanced at them quickly. There were only two for that morning and Tom's was not among them. Breathing a sigh of relief, she replaced the file.

She was standing behind the counter thinking of Tom—and trying not to think of Tom—when Mr. Jones strolled through the doors. He was wearing a blue and white striped seersucker suit, his perpetual bow tie and what looked like a new straw boater. He walked up to the counter and doffed his hat.

"You look mighty pretty this morning, Miss Johnson," he said.

"Thank you. You look very dapper yourself."

"Why, thank you," he said. He looked at her closely. "Do I notice a new gleam in your eyes? Could it be that you are in love?"

Becky blushed. Was it *that* obvious?

"Ah," Mr. Jones said, "I see I have guessed correctly. And who is this young swain?"

Becky smiled at him. He was so incredibly old-fashioned and charming.

"You promise not to tell anybody?" she said, lowering her voice.

"On a stack of bibles."

"He's supposed to stop by here this afternoon."

"Not the young man with the two-wheeled chariot and the mastiff?"

Where did he learn to talk like that, Becky wondered? And how did he know it was Tom? Becky nodded.

"An able-bodied young man," he pronounced. "Interested in . . . ?"

"Physics," Becky supplied.

"Ah, physics. A worthy pursuit. Well, my dear, I shall keep an eagle eye out for this young Adonis. That is," he said, his eyes twinkling, "if I am not, once again, put to sleep by the vagaries of the financial community." With that, he turned and sauntered over to his customary table in the Periodicals department.

Becky watched him as he settled down with the newspaper. What a grand old man, she thought.

Mrs. Francis came out of the office and asked Becky if she could process a few new titles. Becky followed her back to the office. She groaned inwardly when she saw the mountain of books on the spare desk. A few new titles! There must have been a hundred books in the pile.

"They need new cards for the card catalog file," Mrs. Francis explained.

She left Becky to her task. Why today, of all days, did she have to be stuck in the office? Becky asked herself. It would take all afternoon to process all those titles. Reluctantly, she sat down behind the typewriter. Well, it had to be done. She took a book off the shortest pile and opened it to the copyright page. Rolling a three-by-five card into the machine, she began typing. Each book needed three cards—one for the title, one for the author and one for the subject.

Becky began to type frantically, determined to get the job done and get back out into the main room. But what if Tom came while she was in the office? Would he ask for her? Would he look around and, not seeing her, wait for a while? Maybe he would just pick up his new card and his books and go home?

Had Becky built up their brief conversation into more than was really there? Did Tom think she was just a nice little girl who worked at the public library? Someone to help him find the books he wanted and to talk with occasionally when he stopped by?

She replayed their meeting back through her mind. He had asked her her last name. He had seemed interested. Hadn't he? Had she put herself through all the anticipation of the weekend for nothing? Had she plowed through *The Physicists* in vain? One short conversation and a couple of smiles did not a boyfriend make. But what a smile. She remembered the way his lip curled out and the way his blue eyes sparkled.

Becky looked down at the card in the typewriter. She had typed the same information three times. Have I got it bad, she said to herself. Smiling, she pulled the card out of the machine and dropped it in the wastebasket.

Rolling in a fresh card, she set to work again. But the door to the office was open and she kept pausing to listen to the voices outside. Everytime the front doors opened or she thought she heard a voice, she leaned back in her chair and strained her ears toward the door. At one point, she thought she heard the aphids lady but she wasn't sure. A little later, she heard Mr. Jones flirting with Mrs. Francis at the front desk. She could hear Mrs. Francis laughing. Wouldn't it be a hoot if Mr. Jones and Mrs. Francis, whose husband had died a couple of years ago, developed into a twosome? Becky almost cracked up at the idea.

Why, they could all go on double dates together! She and Mrs. Francis could trade girl talk and compare boyfriends. And Tom and Mr. Jones, who had spent some time in the East, could talk about Boston and New England. A double summer romance at the library. What a great idea!

But first, Becky realized, coming back down to earth, a certain young man had to come back to the library. And he had to ask to see Becky Johnson. Arrrr, she grimaced and rolled another card into the typewriter. She opened a fresh book and doggedly began typing the author card.

At three o'clock it was time for her break. She wasn't even halfway finished with the pile of books. She stood up and stretched. She looked down at her skirt. Was it impossibly wrinkled? She brushed out the folds and decided it was all right.

Becky walked out into the library and casually glanced around. The building was almost empty and she didn't see Tom anywhere. She went into the bathroom and combed her hair. Did she still look as good as she did this morning? She decided that she did. She retucked her blouse into her skirt and went back out to the main room.

During her fifteen-minute break, Becky usually strolled down to the drugstore and had a Tab. Sometimes she ran errands or, if a new magazine had just come in, she took it into the office and browsed through it. Today, she walked over to the new fiction section and pretended to look at the new titles. Then she walked over to the Children's department and looked at the display of new biographies she and Mrs. Francis had set up last week. She straightened a couple of books and realized she couldn't see the main library. She hurried over to the Periodicals department and pretended to be interested in a copy of *House and Garden*.

Mr. Jones lowered *The Wall Street Journal* and winked at her. Becky flashed him a smile that asked if he had seen Tom. He shook his head. The minutes crawled by and soon it was time for her to face the typewriter again.

Becky was concentrating so hard on the typing that she didn't hear the noise behind her. Someone had cleared their throat. She whirled around on her swivel chair. Mr. Jones was standing in the doorway. He had a conspiratorial look on his face. He jerked his head toward the main room and did a pantomime of a person riding a bicycle.

Becky stood up. "Thank you," she mouthed silently. He gave her a small salute and sauntered away. Becky was suddenly a bundle of nerves. What was she going to say? What was *he* going to say? Or not say? Did she have time for one more quick check in the mirror? No. She smoothed down her skirt, shook her light brown hair so it fanned out on her shoulders and walked out the door. Her palms were beginning to perspire.

Tom was standing by the display of new fiction. Her heart leapt right into her throat when she saw him. He was wearing chino pants, a blue button-down shirt and penny loafers. He looked incredibly handsome. He's G.Q., Becky thought to herself. (The guys who were foxes and who also were snappy dressers were referred to as G.Q.— after the men's fashion magazine.)

Becky glanced beyond Tom and saw that Maxwell was keeping his usual vigil outside the doors.

Should she waltz right up to Tom and say hello? Or should she march right back into the office and forget the whole thing? Seeing him in "real" clothes, he looked so mature and so . . . so East Coast, she decided. As though he had just stepped off the campus of some Ivy League school.

As she stood there, hesitating, Tom glanced up and saw her. A warm smile creased his face. He walked over to Becky.

"Hi," he said. "I was wondering where you were."

Becky's heart gave another leap. "I've been working on some new titles," she said. "In the back."

"I thought maybe you weren't here today or something."

He had been thinking about her! "Did you get your books?" she managed to ask.

"Yes," he said, indicating a bulging canvas and leather shoulder bag which was lying on a nearby table. "And my very first River Bend Public Library card." He pulled the buff-colored card out of his shirt pocket and held it up proudly.

Becky saw cards just like it a hundred times a day but she admired it for him anyway. After all, none of those other cards belonged to someone like him.

Should she mention that she had read some of his book? Thermonuclear dynamics, relativity and quantum mechanics were not subjects that

Becky was crazy about but she had plowed through a good portion of the book yesterday. It had been pretty tough reading.

"I read a little of *The Physicists,*" she said.

"You did?"

"Not much," she admitted, "but I enjoyed the history parts."

"It's fascinating, isn't it?" Tom said. "The stories of the scientists and how they made the discoveries and . . ."

She had found the scientist's quest and their dedication interesting. As Tom talked about the book, Becky found herself only half listening to him. She was so mesmerized by just standing near him that she couldn't concentrate on his words. His eyes lit up with enthusiasm for the subject. He had removed his hands from his pockets and was holding them in front of him, gesturing to make a point. Becky watched his strong, smooth hands as he illustrated his words.

She realized he had stopped talking. He was smiling at her. Had she looked bored?

"I could talk all day about science," he said. "You shouldn't let me get warmed up."

"It's interesting," she said, "listening to someone who knows something about it."

"I can get a little boring at times."

Could this gorgeous boy ever be boring? Doubtful.

"I better let you get back to work," he said.

No, Becky's mind screamed. Not yet.

Tom ran his hand through the side of his hair. "Well," he said. "Thanks for all your help."

Becky reached up and twisted a button on the front of her blouse. "You're welcome."

Tom hesitated. "It's nice to see you," he said.

41

"Same here." Becky turned to walk away.

"Becky?"

She whirled around.

"Thanks again," he said.

"Sure. Well . . . bye."

"Bye."

Becky turned and walked toward the office. It had not happened. Had he wanted to say something else and not had the courage to say it? It sort of sounded like that. Becky wanted to stay in the main room and watch him leave. To give them a second chance. Maybe he would change his mind and come back. She wanted to see if he would turn and wave again from the doors. But she noticed that Mrs. Francis was watching her. With a sinking heart, Becky headed for the office.

At the door to the office she turned and looked toward the front entrance of the library. All she saw was a flash of red as Maxwell bounded across the sidewalk.

As she sat down at the typewriter, she asked herself if she had been crazy to think that he might ask her out. He probably had some glamorous girl in Boston that he was in love with. How could a guy that good looking not have a girlfriend? Becky Johnson was just a hick librarian in a hick town . . .

Well, she decided, it was a nice try. Another of her impossible crushes that nothing would come of. Just another boy to pine over. But a little spark of hope flared down inside her. Maybe the next time would be the one. He did have to return those books to the library in two weeks . . . she pushed that spark of hope down deep inside her and rolled another card in the typewriter.

It seemed like it took her forever just to type

one card, but slowly she began to make her way through the pile of books.

About twenty minutes later, the phone rang. Mrs. Francis always answered the phone at the main desk so Becky didn't pay much attention to it. Then, the extension next to her buzzed. Startled, Becky picked up the receiver.

"There's a call for you, Becky. On line one."

Calls were permitted at work but Becky did not receive many. It was probably just her mother, or maybe L.W.

"Hello."

"Becky?"

It was Tom.

"I'm sorry to call you at work . . ."

"That's O.K.," she said quickly.

"I thought I'd take Maxwell to the park tomorrow and I wondered if . . . you'd like to come with us?"

"That sounds like fun," she said. Could he hear her heart thudding through the phone?

"Great," Tom said. "I'll pick you up at ten. Oh, I don't know where you live."

Becky gave him her address and directions on how to get there—just in case.

"See you tomorrow," he said.

Becky said goodbye and hung up the phone. She was so excited that she raised her legs off the floor and whirled around on her desk chair, like a little kid on a soda fountain stool. He had asked her out. He had. Well . . . only to the park. But it was a beginning. On her third revolution, she heard someone clear their throat behind her. Mrs. Francis!

She spun around. Mr. Jones was standing in the doorway. He flashed her a questioning thumbs-up signal. Becky almost ran over and hugged him. Instead, she nodded several times and shot a thumbs-up signal back at him. He smiled and put his straw boater on his head. Tapping it jauntily into place, he strolled away.

Tom was picking her up in the morning. Tomorrow morning. She glanced at the clock. It was four o'clock now. Just eighteen hours away.

# 4

**B**ecky was peeping between the living room curtains when Tom pulled up in front of the house. He was driving a Jeep! A cool-looking, bronze-colored Jeep convertible. Maxwell jumped out of the backseat and frolicked around the wheels.

Tom swung down from the driver's side. Becky's heart gave a little leap at seeing him again. Knotted casually around his neck was a dark blue bandanna. His hair was tousled from the wind and he had on a pair of aviator-style sunglasses. As he walked across the yard to the front door, Becky thought that he looked like someone out of a television commercial. Like one of those handsome guys that are always in the Dr. Pepper or the Tab commercials.

She closed the gap in the curtains and waited

for the door bell to ring. She opened the door after the second chime.

"Hi," Tom said, smiling brightly at her.

"Hi," Becky responded. "I'm ready to go." She stepped out onto the stoop and made sure that the latch clicked as she pulled the door closed.

"Good morning, Maxwell," Becky said, when the dog came running up to her. She bent down and scratched his ears. He barked happily and danced away from her.

"He's excited," Tom said. "I think he knows we're going to the park."

Tom opened the door to the Jeep and Becky climbed inside. Maxwell scrambled into the backseat and Tom took his place behind the wheel.

Becky didn't quite know how to begin the conversation. She didn't want to come on too enthusiastically on her first date with Tom. At the same time, she knew that if she didn't say anything, which would be the easiest, she would just sit there like a vegetable.

"Is this your car?" she asked, hoping that the question would get things rolling.

Tom backed the Jeep out of the driveway and they drove out of the small subdivision where Becky lived.

"It's my mother's," he said, "but I get to drive it most of the time. We've got a cabin in Vermont and we use it there in the winter."

Maxwell poked his head between the front seats. Becky reached over and stroked his strong, soft neck.

"I think you've found a new friend," Tom said.

They were driving along the main street of River Bend when Becky spotted L.W. walking down the sidewalk. Becky waved. L.W. stopped and raised her sunglasses onto her forehead. Her mouth dropped open. She closed her mouth and waved back. The Jeep shot by her as Tom shifted gears.

"Who was that?"

"That's one of my best friends," Becky explained. "Her name's Laurie Wilson, but we call her L.W." Becky told Tom about L.W. and Laurie K. and how they had gotten their nicknames and how long they had all been friends. As she talked, her initial nervousness began to disappear. Tom was a good listener and he was interested in her and her friends. She began to relax and enjoy the bright, sunny morning. The sky was clear and azure-colored, the way that only a Midwestern sky could look on a June morning.

The park was three miles from town. With several acres of gently rolling hills, old oak trees, and a small, sparkling lake, it was the perfect place for Maxwell to get some exercise. The best thing about the park this morning, Becky noted, was that they had the whole place to themselves.

Tom parked the Jeep under a tree. Maxwell leapt out of the car and tore across the grass, running with his nose along the ground. Tom and Becky got out and Tom pulled a white Frisbee out of the back.

"Do you know how to use one of these?" he asked, tossing the Frisbee at her.

Becky caught it expertly and, with a deft underhand motion, sailed it back to him.

Tom caught it easily. "You're pretty good."

"I don't spend all my time in the library," Becky said, laughing.

"How'd you get so good?"

"Todd, my little brother, was a Frisbee freak for a while," Becky explained, "and I sort of picked it up." Becky ran across the park. "Throw it," she yelled. Tom sailed the white saucer at her. She darted to her left, jumped high into the air, grabbed at the Frisbee and missed it. Chagrined, Becky picked it up. "I'm a little rusty."

"You just need some practice," Tom said, as he caught the disk and threw it back to her.

They sailed the Frisbee back and forth. The rhythms and the skills of the game came back to Becky and in a few minutes she was tossing it just like an expert. Then Tom started getting fancy. He leapt high into the air and caught it behind his back. Barely touching back down, he zipped the disk back to her. Or, he would raise one leg, catch the Frisbee under his thigh and, whirling around, without missing a beat, send it back to Becky.

Tom paused and whistled loudly between his teeth. Maxwell barked and came bounding out of the woods at the edge of the park.

"Here it comes, buddy," Tom yelled and tossed the Frisbee at the dog.

Maxwell dashed forward, soared into the air and caught the disk in his mouth. He bounded toward Tom. When he was a few feet away, he crouched down next to the grass and looked at Becky and Tom expectantly. His tail was wagging a mile a minute.

"The only problem is trying to get it away from him," Tom said, chuckling.

"C'mon Maxwell," Becky said. "Bring it here." She clapped her hands.

The dog growled playfully and pranced away from her.

"So you want to play," Tom said. He took a low running start, like a defensive lineman, and tried to tackle the dog. Maxwell sidestepped him easily and tore off across the field.

Tom rolled over on the grass and jumped to his feet. "Let's go," he shouted. He and Becky raced after the dog. They chased Maxwell all around the field but couldn't catch him.

Becky paused to catch her breath. Maxwell came over and laid the Frisbee at her feet, as if he were offering her a priceless gift.

"Good dog," she said. She picked up the Frisbee with one hand and patted Maxwell with the other.

They played for about an hour. They tried to play Keep-away-from-Maxwell but he was too good for them. He would spring into the air and catch the bright white disk in mid-flight and then refuse to give it up.

Becky paused to watch Tom as he frolicked with the dog. Tom laughed and talked to Maxwell almost as if he was human; Maxwell yipped and barked as if he was talking back. Tom had the grace and speed of a natural athlete. Becky wondered what sports he had participated in at school.

Maxwell raced away from Tom and came galloping directly at Becky. She imitated Tom's earlier tackle crouch and tried to waylay him. She missed and plopped down on the grass with a thud. Tom ran up to her and, taking her hand, pulled her to her feet.

Still holding her hand, he looked directly at her. His large pupils were the color of a sapphire.

"Thanks," she said, a little uneasily. She

glanced down at her shoes and pulled her hand away from his warm, strong hand.

"I think our star player has given out on us," Tom said, tilting his head to one side.

Becky followed his gaze. Maxwell had lain down under a tree and was trying to gnaw a piece out of the side of the Frisbee.

"He's got the right idea," Becky said.

Tom and Becky settled down in the shade near the dog.

"How are the books you checked out?" Becky asked.

"Pretty good," Tom said. "Especially the one on Einstein."

"Are you getting credit for the course?" Becky didn't know if a high school student could get college credit or not.

"I'm actually just auditing the course," Tom said. "But I may go ahead and write a paper on some aspect of Einstein's studies. I can always use it later." He ran his hand through the side of his hair. "What are you reading?"

It was the first time a guy—a date—had ever asked Becky what she was reading. Should she tell him about Edith Wharton? Would he think she was weird? No, she decided, any guy who read biographies of Albert Einstein would understand. She told him how Mrs. Francis had helped her with a summer reading list, beginning with Edith Wharton's novels.

"I've only read *Ethan Frome*," Tom said, referring to Mrs. Wharton's most famous novel, "but I'm kind of familiar with her work."

"I love *The Age of Innocence*," Becky said. "It's all about society life in New York in the nineteenth century." She went on to tell him how good it felt to have a reading program and how she felt that she was learning something—and enjoying it at the same time.

Tom nodded his head. "That's partly why I decided to audit the course," he said. "That, and because I thought I might meet some new people."

"Do you miss Boston?"

"Yeah," Tom replied. "I'd been there all my life."

"Do you have a lot of friends there?"

"Most of my friends in Boston go away for the summer or they live in New York or Rhode Island. But my best friend, Edge . . ."

"Edge?"

Tom smiled at her. "His name is Malcom Edgington Simpson but we call him Edge. We went to school together and he lives in Boston so we spent a lot of time together. You'd like Edge," Tom said. "He may come to visit in August and you'll get to meet him."

Becky glanced down at her hands. Was Tom just being friendly or did he intend for them to still be seeing each other in August? She hoped it was the latter. Would Edge be like Tom? He would have to be a pretty neat guy if he was Tom's best friend.

Tom explained that he had gone to a private high school in Massachusetts so most of the guys he knew didn't live in Boston or near him at all.

Becky had never known anyone who went to a prep school. Everyone in River Bend went to public school and didn't leave home until they went to college. And a lot of them didn't even do that. They stayed at home and went to the local college, S.I.U. A few, who could afford it, went to Abercrombie. Was going to a private school the reason that Tom seemed so much more confident and mature than the other boys she knew? Becky picked at a blade of grass in front of her. She had never known anyone from the East Coast before and she wasn't sure if that was what made him different or not.

"What's it like? Private school, I mean."

"I liked it," he said. "It's got a great curriculum and I liked most of the other guys." Tom twisted a blade of grass through his fingers. "What's River Bend High like?"

Becky had never had to explain her high school to anyone. Where should she start? She decided to begin with her favorite subject: English. She told him how good the English department was and how much she was looking forward to taking her honors junior English course because the instructor, Mr. Bridges, loved literature and was a good teacher. Also that the Speech department was excellent and always did well at the statewide speech contests.

Becky thought that maybe she had gotten a little carried away with English so she told him about the Student Council—she had been a member for two years already—and about the football and the basketball teams.

"Do you think you'll go out for one of the teams?" she asked.

Tom gave her a wry smile. "The sports were a little different at the school I went to."

Becky looked puzzled. How could basketball and football be different?

"There was kind of a football team," Tom said,

"but they weren't very good. The best team was the rugby team."

"Rugby?"

"Do you know the game?"

"I've heard of it," she said quickly.

"It's like a cross between football and soccer; fast like soccer but with a lot of contact like football. I was on the team." He glanced out at the lake. "I was pretty good." He seemed embarrassed to make that statement but it didn't come out like bragging. "I also played a lot of squash," he continued, "although there isn't a squash team. And a lot of my friends are into sailing—Edge especially."

He sounded like something out of a novel! Rugby, squash, sailing. What was this gorgeous boy doing in River Bend, Illinois? Suddenly, Becky felt incredibly inadequate. Did she look like the original hayseed to him? Like any minute she would don a checked gingham dress and invite him to a square dance or a taffy pull? Well, she reasoned, it wasn't quite that bad, but it sure must seem different to him. Becky shook her hair around her shoulders.

"Edge has a beautiful sailboat," Tom said, "at his parent's summer place on Nantucket Island, so we spent most of the summers sailing. Two years ago we sailed from Nantucket all the way up the coast to Maine. That was incredible."

Becky was raptly listening to Tom, trying to digest all this information.

"Do you sail?" he asked.

Becky grinned. Did anybody from River Bend sail? She couldn't think of anyone. "No," she said. "But it always looked like it was a lot of fun."

"I'm going to miss it." He glanced out at the tranquil surface of the lake again. "Does the high school have a rugby team?"

Becky laughed. "I'm afraid not," she answered, "but maybe you could start one."

Tom smiled at her.

"Are you really going to go to high school here?"

"I want to," he said. "My parents aren't crazy about the idea but I think I can talk them into it."

Becky's heart sank a little. Had she just gotten to know this incredible guy only to have him possibly go away in a short time? It would be so dreamy to have him as a boyfriend next winter. Cool it, she told herself. You've just met Tom and you've practically got yourself going steady with him already.

"I think you'd like the school," she said. "There's a terrific chemistry teacher and I think there are two or three physics courses."

Maxwell hauled himself up and came over and nuzzled Tom's shoulder. Absently, Tom patted the dog's back.

"Somebody," Tom said, pulling his hand away, "has picked up just about every burr in the woods."

He had Maxwell lay down in front of him. Becky scooted over and they began to pick the sticky burrs out of the dog's silky red coat.

"Do you have a bicycle?" Tom asked.

Becky said that she did but admitted that she hadn't ridden it in a long time.

"People don't ride bikes around here much, do they?"

"The little kids do." Then Becky almost blushed.

Tom laughed. "I know what you mean." He tossed a handfull of burrs behind him. "I belonged to a bicycle club in Boston and we used to take weekend trips in New England. Last summer I spent two weeks in Switzerland."

"Switzerland," Becky said. "Really?"

"We started in Germany," Tom explained, "and rode through a valley into the Alps. We didn't climb any mountains until the end."

Becky watched him as he described the beauty of the Swiss countryside.

He was definitely the best looking guy she had ever been out with. Jonathan was cute, handsome even, but he did not possess Tom's classic features. She had an impossible urge to lean over and kiss him. Would that shock him? Was it worth a try? She knew, of course, she would never have the nerve to do it. . . .

Could a guy as smart and as good looking as Tom really be interested in her? In little Becky Johnson? Maybe. She sighed. What a glorious morning, she thought. To be sitting under a tree at the park with this guy who had just walked into her life a few days ago. With a start, she realized that Tom had stopped talking. He was staring at her with a half smile on his face.

"Hello," he said.

"What? I'm sorry."

"What were you thinking about?"

Becky looked down at the dog's shiny dark coat. "I don't think I better tell you."

"C'mon," he prodded, "tell me."

"Well," Becky said, "I was thinking about what a beautiful morning it is."

"Is that all?"

Becky looked into his eyes. "Uh huh," she

replied. She continued to look into his eyes. She wanted to look down, to break the glance, but her eyes were locked in his gaze.

Accidently, their hands touched as they patted Maxwell's back. Becky pulled her hand away quickly.

Tom reached up and adjusted his blue bandanna.

They looked away from each other. Becky was afraid to speak.

Finally, Tom broke the silence. "What do you do in River Bend in the evenings?"

Was he going to ask her out? Or was he just making conversation? "The things kids do everywhere," she answered, comfortable again to look back at him. "Go to the movies, go to parties, go dancing—there's a place in town that has live music on Saturday nights. Go cruising."

"Cruising?"

"You know," she said, "drive around town, see who else is out, talk to the other kids."

"Really?"

"Haven't you ever been cruising?"

"I don't think so," Tom said, "you don't drive around Boston—not if you can help it."

"What do you do in Boston in the evenings?"

"Go to the movies, go to parties," he parroted, smiling at her. "And, well, Edge's grandmother has a box at the opera and my parents like the symphony and my mother was on the board of the art museum and . . . you must think that sounds weird, right?"

Becky shook her head.

"I also ski in the winter and . . ."

Becky was still trying to recover from rugby, squash and sailing. Now, on top of that, here was opera, the symphony, skiing. "Is there anything you don't do?" she blurted.

"What do you mean?"

Now, Becky was embarrassed. "I mean, all that cultural stuff, and all the sports. It's so different from what we do around here."

Tom dismissed it all with a wave of his hand. "It's just around," he said. "It's no big deal."

Well, Becky thought, if he was going to live in River Bend, he would have to get used to doing without some of those activities. "Why don't we go cruising sometime?" she suggested. "You might enjoy it."

"I bet I would." Tom looked at his sporty black wristwatch. "Right now, we better cruise home," he said. "It's almost one o'clock."

Where had the morning gone? Becky wondered. They had been at the park for almost three hours. It seemed like just minutes ago that he had pulled up in his Jeep and swung down to the ground like a young god alighting from a chariot. She smiled to herself. That was Mr. Jones's description.

They piled into the car and headed back to town.

Tom invited her to go bike riding on her next day off. "There's supposed to be a great bike path up by the Mississippi River," he said. "Near Alton."

Becky knew of the path but she had never ridden on it. "What I am going to do with two flat tires?"

"Easy," Tom said. "I'll just take your bike home with me tonight and fix it up."

Becky protested.

"I'd enjoy doing it. When is your next day off?"

"Friday."

"Great. I'll pick you up in the morning. We'll drive up to the beginning of the path and ride all along the mighty Mississippi. You know, I haven't seen the river yet."

"You haven't been properly introduced to the Midwest until you've seen the Mississippi," Becky said.

Tom reached over and took her hand. "I think I'm going to like the Midwest," he said.

5

**B**ecky retied the pale green bandanna around her neck for the third time and stepped back to survey herself in the mirror. Why was it that the bandanna had looked so casual and so right around Tom's neck and looked so klutzy on her? Her dark green tank top and white shorts were the perfect outfit for bicycle riding but she needed an accessory to set off the outfit.

She glanced at the clock on her nightstand. Tom would be there in a few minutes. Reluctantly, she pulled the bandanna from around her neck. Then she had an idea. Rolling the material into a strip, she wrapped it around her neck twice like a choker and tied the ends at the back. Perfect. It was just the right touch.

Becky dashed into the kitchen. Todd was in the family room, sprawled on the couch, watching a rerun of "I Love Lucy." Ethel, Fred and Lucy were dressed up like hillbillies and any minute Ricky was going to come home with an important Broadway producer and the Mertzes and Lucy would make gigantic fools of themselves. Becky and Todd knew all the shows by heart but they could still watch them over and over. This morning, however, she didn't have time to enjoy their antics.

Becky checked the contents of the picnic lunch that she had stowed inside Todd's backpack earlier in the morning. At first, she had worried about what to take. She couldn't decide whether she should try and pack an elegant little picnic or maybe make something unusual. She didn't know enough about Tom yet to know what kind of food he liked to eat. Then she had decided that simple was best. She had packed three thick ham and cheese sandwiches—three because guys were always hungry, a bunch of fresh, green grapes, several ripe, magenta-colored plums, corn chips and two cans of juice. And for dessert, four Hershey's bars: two plain, two with almonds. What was a picnic without chocolate bars?

Everything in the backpack was in order.

"Can I have a sandwich?" Todd called from the family room.

"For breakfast?"

"Breakfast, lunch, brunch," he intoned. "I'm hungry."

"You'll have to make it yourself."

"Aw," he whined, "make it for me. You make the best ham sandwiches in the whole world."

Becky looked across the counter at him. Any fool could make ham sandwiches. Todd was trying hard to keep a straight face. She pretended to consider the compliment.

"And you're so pretty too," he said. "Probably the prettiest sister in all of River Bend." He glanced at the TV screen, then back at Becky. "Besides, I let you borrow my backpack."

"On one condition."

Todd was suddenly suspicious. "Forget it," he said. "I'll make it myself."

"Promise you won't embarrass me in front of Tom."

"Aw, Marion," he said, "when did I ever embarrass you?"

"About every twenty minutes."

"All right. I promise."

Becky slapped together a sandwich and carried it over to Todd. She set it down on his stomach and sat herself down on a footstool to watch TV.

A few minutes later there was a knock on the family room door. Todd jumped up and opened the door.

"Hi," Becky heard Tom say, "you must be Todd."

"The one and only. I bet you're Tom."

The one and only, Becky thought.

Todd held open the screen door and Tom came in. Tom looked incredible. He had on a yellow shirt with black and white stripes around the sleeves, a pair of official black bicyclist shorts and black bicycle shoes.

"Wow," Todd exclaimed, "you look just like that guy out of that movie. You know, the one about the guy who was a bicycle freak. And what a cool-looking cap."

Tom was wearing a racer's cap. It was made of white canvas and had black Italian lettering on the sides and on the bill.

"Would you like one?"

"Yeah," Todd's eyes lit up.

"I've got a couple of extra ones at home," Tom said. "I'll bring you one."

Becky knew what Todd's next question was going to be. She held her breath.

"When?"

Tom smiled at him. "The next time I come to pick Becky up," he replied.

Becky let her breath out slowly. She'd get Todd for that one. But, at least, Tom's answer was reassuring.

"Cool," Todd said, "thanks."

Becky got the backpack off the kitchen counter. "I'm ready," she said.

Tom took the backpack from her. "What a nice house," he said.

"It's sort of messy."

"It looks fine," he said.

Todd came to the screen door and watched them as they got into the Jeep. "Bye Tom," he called. "Don't let her fall off her bicycle."

That was number two, Becky thought. Tom just laughed and waved goodbye as he backed the car out of the driveway.

Becky looked at her bicycle in the back. "Thanks for fixing up my bike. You didn't have to clean it up too."

"It was no trouble at all," Tom replied.

Becky couldn't think of anything else to say. There were lots of things she wanted to say, like how great he looked, and how happy she was, and how, if those dark clouds over in the west turned to rain, she was going to kill herself, but she wasn't quite sure where to begin.

"Why don't you put a tape in the player," Tom said, "they're in the glove compartment."

Becky opened the compartment and looked through the cassettes. There were several Beatles tapes, two Doors tapes and three that were marked *Tosca* that had been recorded at home. What was *Tosca?* she wondered. A New Wave band? Becky picked "Sgt. Pepper" and slipped it into the player. The wonderful sounds of The Fab Four filled the air.

In a little while they had driven through Alton and were at the beginning of the bike path. Tom parked at the side of the road and lifted the bicycles out of the back. His bike had a bright orange touring bag attached to the handlebars and a plastic bottle full of water hooked to the front vertical bar.

The sun was shining now. The sky was a golden blue and the clouds looked like they would blow away eventually. There were a few pleasure boats on the Mississippi, several sailboats and far up-stream, a giant barge was lazily floating toward them.

"I think the path goes for about twenty or thirty miles," Tom said. "Shall we ride along until we get tired? And then stop for lunch?"

"Sounds fine to me."

Tom settled the backpack across his shoulders. They mounted their bicycles and set off. The path was a strip of smooth asphalt about six feet wide that ran along the base of the limestone and tree-covered bluffs. Since Tom and Becky were the only ones there, they rode side by side.

"Why is the town called River Bend," Tom asked, "if it's fifteen miles from the river?"

Becky knew the answer to his question. "The town's not that old," she said, "but evidently, during prehistoric time, they think the river actually did come close to where the town is now. That's how it got its name."

A comfortable silence settled over them as they pedalled lazily along. The path was almost flat, which pleased Becky because she didn't think she was ready for cross-country touring—yet. Occasionally the path curved inward and they would ride from the bright, warm sunshine into the dark green shade of the overhanging tree branches. Close to the bluff they could hear the sounds of the birds and the rustlings of small animals. There was hardly any traffic on the river road, which was on their left, and it seemed to Becky that the world belonged to just her and Tom.

Once, when they were riding close together, Tom reached over and put his hand on Becky's shoulder. "I'm glad we're doing this," he said, smiling a genuine, appreciative smile at her.

Becky almost lost control of the bike.

"Did I startle you?"

"No," she managed to say. "I'm glad we're here too."

After about an hour and a half, Tom suggested that they stop and rest. They parked the bikes under a tree and got off and stretched.

"Hey," Tom said, "why don't we climb up the bluff and have lunch up there?" He was pointing at a limestone overhang halfway up the side of the bluff.

"That's a great idea."

Tom unhooked the canvas bag from his handlebars and slung it over his shoulder. "Snakebite kit," he said, patting the bag.

Becky's eyes widened noticeably.

"I'm just kidding."

"Are you sure?"

Tom nodded, smiling.

Slowly, they made their way up the side of the bluff. It was steep in places so they had to make sure they had careful footholds and once in a while they had to grasp a root or a branch in order to pull themselves up.

Finally, they came to the wide ledge that Tom had pointed out. It was covered with dark green moss and sweet smelling grass. Tom pulled a small canvas sheet out of his bag and spread it out.

The river looked as though it were ten stories below them. Becky hadn't realized how high they had climbed. "We can see the whole world from up here," she said, exulting in the view.

"Isn't it beautiful. Look how tiny the sailboats are."

They sat down and watched the lazy river. Tom put his arm around Becky's back. His touch sent tingles along her spine. Was he going to kiss her? Right here, in front of the whole world? She hoped he would but she was a little nervous about it.

"Are you hungry?" she asked suddenly. Then she could have kicked herself. Why had she spoiled the moment?

"I could eat a horse," he said, "or maybe a nice, young librarian." He leaned over and nibbled at her shoulder.

"How about a ham sandwich?" Becky said quickly. Maybe she better be careful. Here she was, all alone, halfway up a mountain, with a guy she really didn't know very well. Maybe they did things a lot quicker in Boston than they did in River Bend.

Becky laid the picnic out on the sheet. She handed Tom a sandwich.

As they ate, Tom talked about the sailboats, describing the various sails and conjecturing on how fast they would go, and which ones he would like to take her out on. He was surprised at the beauty of the river. It was, he told her, just as awesome, in its way, as the Atlantic.

"What a great picnic," Tom said, finishing off his second chocolate bar.

It began to sprinkle. The rain took them by surprise.

"Never fear," Tom said, opening up his shoulder bag. He pulled out a large plastic poncho. He shook it out, gave one corner to Becky to hold, took the other corner in his right hand, and sat down beside her, pulling the poncho over them.

The warm rain drummed softly on the top of their improvised tent. Tom put his arm around Becky's waist and pulled her close to his side. The wet trees and the damp earth smelled fresh and clean and new to Becky. She closed her eyes. She felt Tom's strong arm tighten around her and she leaned closer to him, resting her cheek on his shoulder. She never wanted this moment to end. She wanted to remember everything just the way it was: the smell of the rain-washed woods and earth, the warmth of Tom's body next to hers, the feel of his breathing as his shoulder rose and fell almost imperceptibly against her cheek.

Becky opened her eyes. Tom was watching her.

"You're beautiful," he said softly.

Becky looked into his eyes and was lost for an instant, an eternity, in their smoky blue depths.

He lowered his hand from the poncho and touched a damp lock of her hair which had escaped from her ponytail. Then he leaned toward her and put his lips on hers. Becky closed her eyes and gave herself up to the excitement of their first kiss. She let go of the poncho and put her hand on his shoulder and held him tight, gently caressing the soft cotton of his shirt. The voluminous poncho settled around them like a cocoon, wrapping them in a tender, shadowy warmth, blotting out everything but the feel of his lips lingering on hers.

Tom broke the kiss and lightly grazed the end of Becky's chin with his lips. Becky opened her eyes.

"Could you tell me," he whispered, "where the Biography section is?"

Becky smiled. "Perhaps," she whispered.

Tom moved his lips to the side of her hair and softly kissed her ear. He continued to hold her close, his arms around her, one hand gently tangled in the damp curls at the back of her neck.

"I think it's stopped raining," he said softly. He peered out a corner of the poncho and reported that the sun was shining.

Becky raised the poncho over her head. She felt like a new butterfly. A pale, trembling butterfly who was seeing the world for the first time. And the world was fresh and young again, eternal. The sun was beaming and the sky was clear and rain-washed; the river beneath it flowed dark and sparkling.

Tom stood up and held out his hand to her. Becky took it and stood up next to him.

"I've been wanting to kiss you ever since that first day at the library," he said.

"I've been wanting to kiss you too," Becky murmured.

"Do you think we could do it one more time?" he asked, smiling down at her.

Becky put her arms around his neck. Tom

leaned down and, once again, pressed his lips to hers. He laid his cheek along the side of her head. "Marion the librarian," he murmured.

Becky was surprised. "How did you know that?"

"I just thought of it. Why?"

"My brother calls me that."

"Do you mind?"

How could she mind? "I have a name for you too," she said, teasing him.

"What?"

"It's pretty juvenile."

"Tell me."

"Tom Terrific."

"That sounds like a lot of responsibility."

"He's a character in a series of cartoons," Becky explained, "who has this magic hat that can do all kinds of tricks and . . . you don't mind, do you?"

"How could anyone mind being called Tom Terrific."

They turned and gazed down at the river.

"Well," Tom said, at last, "I better put on my magic hat and get us home. Have you seen my Tom Terrific hat—by the way?"

"I think you left it in the Jeep."

"I did? I'm always doing that." He scratched his head. In that case, I guess we'll just have to climb down this cliff."

They gathered together the remains of the picnic and put everything back in the pack. They scooted down the face of the bluff and were soon beside their bicycles.

Becky paused and looked out at the wide, mysterious river. "What a perfect summer afternoon," she sighed.

"'Summer afternoon, summer afternoon'," Tom quoted. "'The two most beautiful words in the English language'."

"How lovely," Becky cried. "What's it from?"

"Henry James," Tom said. "I read it somewhere. It's from a letter he wrote to Edith Wharton."

Edith Wharton! Becky loved Tom more in that instant than she had ever loved anyone in her entire life.

"What is it?" he asked anxiously, seeing the look on Becky's face.

"Edith Wharton. Remember."

Suddenly, he looked very shy. "Of course I remember," he said.

Becky was touched and flattered by the quotation. So moved, in fact, that she thought she might cry. Which was really dumb. Tom must have noticed because he said, "We better get going. We've got quite a few miles to cover." He busied himself getting their bikes ready.

They climbed on their bicycles and rode back along the path. The wind felt cool and refreshing on Becky's face. If anyone had told her, two weeks ago, she thought, that she would be riding along the River Road bike path on her bicycle, and having one of the best days of her life, she would have told them that they were crazy.

Becky watched Tom who was riding in front of her. He was bent over the handlebars, the muscles of his back rippling under his shirt, the muscles of his long legs pushing rhythmically against the pedals.

"Summer afternoon, summer afternoon," her heart sang all the way back to the car.

Once they were in the Jeep and back on the road, Tom asked Becky if she liked opera.

"I don't know anything about it," she admitted.

"I don't know much," he said. "I've sort of picked it up by osmosis. There's a tape in the glove compartment," he continued, "*Tosca*, sung by Pavarotti. Why don't you play the third tape."

So that's what *Tosca* is, Becky thought, as she located the tape and slipped it in the machine. Becky really didn't know anything about opera. In fact, she had never even considered listening to it before. Opera was simply something that the family flipped the dial past on the TV whenever the Metropolitan Opera was shown on the public television station.

An incredible tenor voice leapt out of the speakers at them. The music sounded sweet and beautiful. And sort of sorrowful.

"It's an Italian opera," Tom explained. "Written by Puccini. We really shouldn't start at the end but I want you to hear Pavarotti's aria. It's sung almost at the end when the guy says goodbye to Tosca, the main character, right before she kills herself."

Tom reached over and turned up the volume. "This is it," he said, "coming up."

One of the most beautiful solos Becky had ever heard filled the air. The voice rose in a bright, mournful curve. The orchestra, in the background, swelled delicately behind the notes. Pavarotti hit an incredibly beautiful high note, held it, paused and hit it again. The orchestra crashed dramatically behind the voice and Becky's soul seemed to rush out of her, seemed to soar up into the clouds and hover, like a mist, on the sounds of the notes that were still quivering in the air. She shivered.

"Isn't it incredible?" Tom said.

Becky could only nod her head.

"Want to listen to it again?"

"Could we?"

"Sure."

Becky rewound the tape and started it over again. "I never knew it could be so beautiful," she said.

"It's not all like this," Tom said.

As they entered the outskirts of River Bend, the music swelled once again and they were transported back in time, caught up in the tragic fate of the lovers in the opera. At a stoplight, they got a funny look from the guy in the car next to them. Becky giggled. Tom just nodded at the guy and tipped his hat.

Tom was full of surprises, Becky thought, as they pulled into the driveway of her house. He seemed to know so much. And he wasn't pompous about any of it, it just seemed to be woven into the fabric of his life.

Becky watched him as he lifted her bicycle down and leaned it against the side of the garage.

"I had a wonderful time," Becky said.

"Me too." He climbed back behind the wheel of the Jeep. "Maybe we could do it again."

"I'd like that."

"I'll call you," he said, as he started the engine.

She floated into the house. Nobody was home as she drifted through the family room and into the kitchen. She laid the backpack on the counter. Pavarotti's aria came drifting back into her mind. She decided to look over the family's record collection and see if there might be some opera there. In the family room, Becky carefully flipped through her parent's albums. There were lots of Peter, Paul and Mary albums—her mother had been a folk music fan when she was young: Bob Dylan, Joan Baez, several Broadway cast recordings, soundtracks to movies and a collection of Christmas carols that her grandmother had given her and Todd. That was it. No opera.

Nobody in the family was really big on music. Except the rock and roll that she liked to listen to on the radio. But the library had a big record collection. Becky would check out several operas, she decided, and learn some more about this new area of music that Tom had just introduced her to.

The phone rang. Becky was still sort of floating around the room when she answered it.

"Have I got some news," L.W. burbled.

"What?"

"News," L.W. repeated, "about Tom. And the Stearns."

"Tom?"

"You know. The guy you spent the day with!"

"Oh sure," Becky said dreamily.

"Can I come over?"

"News about the Stearns!" Becky yelped. "What?"

"I'm glad to know you're still with us," L.W. said. "I'll be right over."

Becky hung up the phone. What could L.W. have found out about Tom? And how could she have found it out?

Becky didn't have long to wait.

"Now you know I don't like gossip," L.W. said as she breezed in the door and threw herself on the couch. "But this isn't really gossip. It's more informational."

"What is it?" Becky asked, concern showing in her voice.

"It's not bad," L.W. said, "calm down." She drew her knees up under her chin. "Mrs. Middleman, at the real estate office—who sold the Stearns' their house—is friendly with Mom. And she found out quite a bit about them. She told Mom everything this morning at the A & P."

Had something terrible happened to them in Boston that forced them to leave and move to Illinois?

L.W. launched into her tale. It turned out that Mrs. Stearns was from a wealthy, old-line Boston family. Lots of money and prestige. Very upper, upper. Mr. Stearns, whose family hadn't been in Boston nearly as long, was also wealthy. Unfortunately, his father had lost most of the family fortune during the Depression.

Becky knew that the Stearns were well off but she didn't know they had *that* kind of money.

L.W. was continuing her report. "Mr. Stearns studied at Oxford University—in England—after he graduated from Harvard and is considered a brilliant scholar and historian." L.W. shifted her position on the couch. "He was the head of the history department at a small college near Boston. Mrs. Middleman doesn't know which one. Evidently, he couldn't pass up the opportunity to become the president of Abercrombie, even though Mrs. Stearns hated to leave Boston."

"Wow," Becky said, trying to digest all the data.

"Mrs. Middleman said that Mrs. Stearns is nice, but distant," L.W. reported. "Mr. Stearns, however, is genial and very outgoing. And supposedly very handsome. And," L.W. paused dramatically, "they paid cash for the house!" She named the price. The number had six figures in it.

"I don't know what to say," Becky stammered. "I didn't know they had that kind of a background. I mean, Tom seems so nice and easygoing and . . ."

"And gorgeous."

Becky nodded absently. "He seems to know about a lot of things that I don't know about but I just assumed that was because he was from a big city. Sort of."

"Well, Becky," L.W. said, leaning toward her, "you've got yourself a real society boyfriend."

"Wow," Becky said again.

"Wow is right," L.W. echoed. She put her feet down on the floor. "How was your bike trip?"

Becky was still trying to take in all the new information about the Stearns. "What?"

L.W. repeated her question.

Becky pulled her hair out of the ponytail and shook her hair around her shoulders. "Incredible," she said. She told L.W. about the kiss, the quote from Henry James and the opera music.

"It sounds heavenly," L.W. said. "Now why can't I find a boyfriend with some brains—and a bike!"

"You will," Becky reassured her.

"I hope so," L.W. said. "Laurie K.'s got Jeff, well—part of the time; and you've got Tom."

"I don't have him," Becky protested. "We've only been out twice."

"Did he ask you out again?"

"He said he'd call."

"I hope he does."

"Me too."

L.W. glanced at the wall clock above the

television. "I've got to go," she said. She stood up.

Becky followed her to the door. "Maybe we better not tell Laurie K. about this," she said, feeling disloyal to her other friend.

"Why not?"

"You know how she is," Becky said. "She'd think Tom was stuck-up or something."

L.W. concurred. "You may be right. I'll call you later," she said, as she headed for her convertible.

Becky closed the door. She felt as though she were in shock. After the wonderful afternoon, now to find out that Tom and his family were part of society. "Society?" It wasn't a word that was used very much in River Bend.

## 6

"You're up early," Mrs. Johnson said when Becky came into the kitchen. She was dressed for work and was just finishing a cup of coffee.

"I'm going to help Tom pick out the new paint for his room," Becky told her. "And help him paint."

"What about the library?"

"I'm off today."

Her mother slowly put down her coffee cup. "Becky," she said, "I don't want to sound like a prude but I don't think you should spend the whole day at Tom's house alone with him."

"Oh Mom," Becky said. "We're going to be painting his room."

"I'm serious," Mrs. Johnson said. "Are his parents going to be home?"

"I suppose his mother will be there," Becky answered.

"You can go with him to pick out the color," she said, "but if no one else is home, I would prefer that you not stay."

"You've met Tom," Becky said. "You know what a nice guy he is."

"He seems like a very nice young man, but . . ."

"Oh Mom," Becky said again, "you act like we're going to be . . . going to be . . ."

"Going to be what?"

"Never mind," Becky said.

"That," her mother said, standing up from the table, "is exactly my point."

"You act like you don't trust me."

"Of course we trust you," her mother said, bending over to kiss her on the forehead. "I just don't think it's a good idea for you to be alone all day in a boy's bedroom."

Mrs. Johnson picked up her purse. "Now promise me that if no one is home, you won't stay."

"I promise," Becky said reluctantly.

"Thank you." She found her car keys and walked through the family room on her way to the door. "Goodbye, Todd," she said, "have a good time at the pool."

"Bye," Todd mumbled, not looking up from the rerun of the show that he was watching on television.

Becky heard the door slam. What a drag, she thought. Here I am fifteen, almost sixteen—practically grown-up—and I can't spend an afternoon alone with a boy at his house. She opened the refrigerator door and stared glumly at its well-stocked blue and white interior. There was a big bowl of lasagne left over from last night's dinner. Maybe she would heat that in the microwave and eat it for breakfast. Or, there was one big chunk of chocolate cake left. How would cake and a Coke be for breakfast?

Mrs. Johnson hated it when Becky and Todd ate something bizarre for breakfast. Becky was just upset enough to do something dumb in order to get back at her mother.

"You're air-conditioning the house," Todd said, from behind her, indicating the open refrigerator door.

"Buzz off, Toad."

"Boy, are you in a bad mood."

"I am not in a bad mood," Becky yelled, as Todd retreated back to the family room.

Why was she screaming at Todd? It wasn't his fault. As she started to lift the cake out of the icebox, Becky realized that it wasn't anybody's fault. Her parents cared about her and didn't really monitor her life too much. No more than normal parents did. Though not letting her help Tom paint his room alone was going a little far, Becky thought; in fact, it was downright Victorian. But Tom's mother would probably be there.

"I'm sorry," she called to Todd. Becky put the chocolate cake back in the refrigerator and decided to have a bowl of cereal instead.

She sat down at the table to eat and wondered what Mrs. Stearns was like. She was certainly about to find out—if she was home.

Becky finished her cereal and put her bowl in the dishwasher. She took a quick shower and dressed in a pair of cutoffs and a St. Louis Cardinals T-shirt. She knew she looked a little grubby but they were going to be painting. She hoped. She applied a light coat of lipstick and a smudge of mascara.

She went outside and sat down on the stoop to wait for Tom. Becky still couldn't quite believe that a guy like Tom had picked her to be his girlfriend. He was such a beautiful guy. Maybe she shouldn't think of him as beautiful. No, it was O.K. He wasn't pretty-beautiful because he was much too masculine for that. He was just, well, beautiful-beautiful. All the way around.

They had been going out for over two weeks and it had been the best two weeks of Becky's life. They had gone to an exhibit of Renaissance drawings at the Art Museum in St. Louis, had gone to a showing of *Citizen Kane*—the classic American movie—at Abercrombie and Tom had treated her to a Japanese dinner.

Becky's head felt, at times, like it was spinning with all the dazzling new activities and information that Tom kept introducing her to. In contrast, when she had been dating Jonathan, they had gone to basketball games. She had gone to the games while he played, they had gone out for pizza and had gone to see a Clint Eastwood movie. And they had hung out with the other kids. She wondered if Tom would enjoy just hanging out? Maybe when she got to know him a little better she would show him more of the things that kids in River Bend did.

Painting his room was a pretty common activity, she decided. She would be on safe ground there and wouldn't have to worry about knowing the name of a seventeenth century artist, or the films of a famous American director, or what nouvelle cuisine was.

Tom roared around the corner in the Jeep. He stopped in front of the house and swung down from the driver's side. He was dressed in his usual outfit: rugby shirt and cutoffs. He must have an inexhaustible supply of those striped shirts, Becky thought. Maxwell jumped out of the car and came loping up the yard to Becky.

Becky took Maxwell's head between her hands and gave him a good double scratch behind the ears. Then she ran down the yard to meet Tom. Her Tom.

"It's really great of you to help me paint," Tom said, as he turned the Jeep toward downtown River Bend. "I was sort of hoping that you would offer."

"I don't mind at all," Becky said. "It'll be fun to see your room."

"There's not much there right now," Tom said. He gave her a wicked-looking smile. "But what if I grab you and won't let you out?"

"I would defend my honor to the death," Becky said, putting one hand over her heart and trying to sound like a romantic heroine. Then she couldn't help herself and laughed.

Tom laughed and put his arm around her shoulders. "You're safe with me," he said, smiling his wonderful, clear smile. "Besides, my mother's going to be home all day."

At least the chaperone question was settled, Becky thought.

Tom removed his arm from around her in order to shift into a lower gear and pull into Kaynor's parking lot.

Inside Kaynor's Paint and Wallpaper Store, Laurie K. was arranging a display of varnish cans. Becky had warned her that they were coming but she did a double take when Becky and Tom walked in the front door. She had heard every detail—almost every detail—of Tom and Becky's romance but she hadn't met Tom yet.

Laurie K. put down a can and came forward to greet them. "Can I help you?" she said, in her best store-owner voice.

Becky introduced her to Tom.

"I've heard so much about you from Becky," Tom said. "It's great to finally meet you."

"Me too," Laurie K. replied.

Becky felt that incredible sense of pride that people always feel when they introduce two of their friends to each other. She hoped that Tom and Laurie K. would hit it off.

"What a great store," Tom commented.

He couldn't have said anything better to break the ice with Laurie K. She took a real pride in Kaynor's, especially since she had decided, just last winter, to eventually take over the management of the store from her parents. Her older brother was going to be a lawyer and wasn't interested in the family business. Laurie K., who was good with people and had a natural business sense, had made up her mind to stay in River Bend and continue with the store her grandfather had started.

"Thanks," Laurie K. responded. "What color are you going to paint your room?"

"How did you know I was going to paint my room?" Tom asked.

Laurie K. flashed him a mischievous grin. "Just a wild guess."

Tom smiled at Becky. "Blue," he said to Laurie K.

"Come and look at the paint samples," she suggested and led them to the back of the store where a vast array of tiny color chips were displayed.

Becky helped Tom decide on a pale blue almost the same color as his eyes.

While Laurie K. was getting the paint ready, Tom went off to the front of the store to get an extra brush.

"What a fox," Laurie K. hissed at Becky. "Those eyes and that smile and," she glanced across the store at Tom, "those shoulders."

"I told you."

"I thought you were exaggerating," Laurie K. said as she set the mixed cans of paint on the counter. "Hmmmm," she said, "maybe I'll dust off *my* bicycle."

"Don't you dare," Becky laughed. "You've got Jeff."

"Jeff!" Laurie K. said disgustedly. "I never want to see him again."

Becky was used to this. Laurie K. and Jeff spent more time about to break up or about to get back together than they did actually together.

Tom came up then so Becky didn't get to hear the latest installment in the continuing saga of Jeff and Laurie K. Tom charged the paint to his mother's account and told Laurie K. how nice it was to meet her.

"I liked her," Tom said, when they were back in the Jeep and on the way to his house.

"She liked you too," Becky said.

"I'm glad," Tom said. "Sometimes people's friends don't get along."

"You've been a big hit so far," Becky said.

"How could I not like your friends," he said, reaching over to squeeze her hand.

Becky felt a flutter of anxiety when they

reached the Stearns' house. Now, she had to pass the parent test.

She took a deep breath and followed Tom into the kitchen. The room was enormous and looked like a kitchen out of an interior decoration magazine.

"Mom," Tom called, "we're home."

Mrs. Stearns walked into the kitchen. She was tall and slim. She had short, straight blond hair that framed a set of high cheekbones and a pair of eyes just like Tom's. Even though she was dressed in slacks and a button-down shirt, she was wearing a single strand of pearls and small gold earrings.

"You must be Becky," she said, advancing across the room. Her smile was warm but reserved. "It's so generous of you to offer to help Tom," Mrs. Stearns said. "We had the painters in for the rest of the house, of course, but Tom hated the color I chose and insisted on repainting it himself."

"Is Dad here?" Tom asked, saving Becky the need to think of a reply.

"He's in the library."

The library! The Johnsons had a family room; the Stearns had a library.

"I want Becky to meet him."

"Did I hear someone talking about me?" a deep, rich baritone voice said from the doorway. Mr. Stearns came into the kitchen. He was taller than Tom and had the same dark, straight hair. He was going gray at the temples and had a full, dark beard that gave him an air of authority.

Tom introduced them.

"I understand you work at the library," Mr. Stearns said. "That must be a delightful job."

"I really enjoy it," Becky answered. She felt timid around the Stearns. They didn't seem like real parents. They looked more like a casting director's idea of the ideal couple. She thought any minute someone was going to say, "Roll 'em," and start the cameras turning.

Tom came to her rescue. "We better get started," he said.

"We're so pleased Tom is making new friends in River Bend," Mrs. Stearns said. "Won't you stay for lunch, Becky?"

Becky thanked her and said that she would.

Maxwell was scratching at the back door, asking to be let in. Tom opened the door for him. He followed Becky and Tom down a short hall and up the back stairs to the second floor. There was a pile of boxes sitting on the landing and several packing crates stacked in an empty room. The walls of the hallway were lined with framed prints and a number of oil paintings. Becky was fascinated. She wanted to see everything, to poke her head into every room and find out as much about Tom as she could but Tom led her straight to the end of the hall and to his room.

The walls of his room were painted a dark beige and he had already moved most of the furniture out.

Becky noticed two black-and-white photographs hanging above his desk and a small color photograph sitting on top of the desk. One of the photographs was of a sports team grouped around an ornate silver trophy. Becky picked Tom out immediately.

"That's the rugby team," he explained. "We were the champions last season."

Tom unhooked the smaller picture from the wall and handed it to her.

"What a great picture," Becky exclaimed. It was a five-by-seven of Tom and Maxwell. They were both in midair. Tom was just about to catch a Frisbee. Maxwell, directly in front of him, had leaped into the air and was trying to intercept the Frisbee.

"My brother, Randolph, took it," Tom said. "He's an amateur photographer. Tom picked up the small photo from the desk and pointed to the younger of the two guys, "This is Randolph."

He had talked about his brothers but Becky had never seen a photograph of them. She took the picture from him. The younger boy, a smaller version of Tom, was trying to look serious but there was an impish quality that was struggling to break through his features.

"He's fourteen," Tom said. "He's the brain in the family. Randolph just graduated from high school . . ."

"At fourteen?"

Tom nodded. "And he starts Harvard in the fall. He's there this summer taking introductory classes."

"Wow," Becky said.

"He's brilliant," Tom said. "Loves mathematics. And, right at the moment, I think he's also into Indiana Jones."

Becky was impressed.

"This is Edward?" she asked, remembering the older boy's name.

"Yes. He's twenty. Edward goes to Juilliard, the music school in Manhattan. He's a cellist. This summer he's in England studying string music—Dowland, Vivaldi, that crowd."

Becky didn't know Dowland but she thought she had heard of Vivaldi.

There was a note of flatness in Tom's voice when he talked about Edward. "Don't you get along?"

"We get along all right," Tom said, "it's just that Edward is so serious. He doesn't have much of a sense of humor. Music is pretty serious, I guess. And very competitive. He wants to be a concert cellist," Tom paused and studied the picture. "Randolph is my favorite."

"He looks like a neat kid."

"He is."

Becky didn't know quite what to say about the Stearns. They all seemed so intelligent and involved. All of them doing something, pursuing something. They seemed to know what they wanted and how they were going to get it. "What an impressive family," Becky said.

"We're just your basic group of over-achievers," Tom said.

Becky looked at him quickly. There was a hint of sarcasm in his voice that she didn't understand. "What do you mean?"

"Sometimes we're all so darned focused," Tom started, "everybody running around studying math or making music or studying physics—that sometimes I just want to get in the Jeep with Maxwell and drive off into the sunset. Go someplace far away and just sit in the woods . . ."

Becky had never heard Tom talk like that before and was shocked by the note of bitterness that had crept into his voice. She knew that middle children were supposed to be the ones that had it rough in a family but Tom had seemed so free of all those pressures. Did he feel squeezed by his family? With Randolph on one end and Edward on the other, did he feel obligated to carve out a niche for himself, to create a space separate from theirs?

He looked embarrassed by his outburst.

"But we all have fantasies like that," Becky said. "When I was reading Agatha Christie I desperately wanted to go off to a tiny English village and just sit around all day and drink tea and solve mysteries like Miss Marple."

Tom didn't respond to her analogy. "But you're going to be a physicist," Becky said.

Tom smiled. "Right now, I'm going to be a painter." He leaned down and kissed Becky quickly, brushing his lips across hers. "I'm glad you're here."

Becky wanted him to kiss her again. She wanted to wrap her arms around his waist and hug him tight and tell him not to worry about the family and reassure him that he was wonderful. But she remembered her breakfast time conversation with her mother. "We better get started," she said, indicating the unopened cans of paint.

Tom started rolling the white paint on the ceiling and Becky, who was better with a brush, began to paint carefully around the woodwork. He brought in a small radio and they listened to a St. Louis station that played a good mix of new rock and roll and classics from the Sixties and the Seventies.

They were painting away and singing along with the music when Mrs. Stearns called them to lunch. They were almost finished with the first coat.

Becky wasn't really looking forward to the meal but she decided that it couldn't be that bad. It was only lunch.

"Would you like to see the house?" Mrs. Stearns asked Becky as she met them at the bottom of the stairs.

"I'd love to."

Tom tagged along as Mrs. Stearns lead Becky first into the library. The walls were covered with floor-to-ceiling bookcases. The shelves were filled with leather-bound books. The ceiling was painted a dark green color which perfectly matched the color in the rug that was placed in front of the fireplace. There was a comfortable couch and two large leather-covered wing chairs.

"This is more like a den," Mrs. Stearns explained. "I'm going to make a small office for Martin in one of the rooms at the back of the house."

Becky would have liked to stay and browse among the books but Mrs. Stearns led them into the dining room. The walls were covered with a pale green silk and there was an enormous mahogany table and eight chairs directly in the middle of the room.

"The chandelier is from my Grandmother Remmington's house in Boston," Mrs. Stearns told Becky. "It fits the room nicely, don't you think?"

"It's beautiful," Becky exclaimed.

"Next stop," Tom said, "the living room."

They crossed the wide front hall and entered the living room. Becky had never seen a more beautiful room. There was a baby grand piano in one corner and an antique secretary in another.

Scattered casually across the large oriental rug that covered the floor, were brocade-covered couches and delicately carved wooden tables and chairs. The walls were hung with sketches and oil paintings and everywhere there were beautiful Chinese bowls and vases.

But the most arresting feature of the room was an oil painting of an aristocratic looking woman that was hung above the fireplace.

"That's Grandmother Remmington," Mrs. Stearns said, indicating the painting. "It's a Sargent."

"Who?" Becky asked.

A flicker passed across Mrs. Stearns' eyes. "It was painted by John Singer Sargent," Mrs. Stearns explained, "when Grandmother was in her thirties."

The woman in the painting was seated in a small chair. She was wearing a silver-colored ball gown and the painter had captured every fold and tuck of the lustrous material that cascaded over her knees and trailed along the floor.

"He was a famous portrait painter," Tom said matter-of-factly, leading Becky up closer to the painting.

"Grandmother gave her collection to the Boston Museum," Mrs. Stearns said, as if people gave away art collections every day, "but I insisted that we keep the portrait in the family."

"It's beautiful," Becky said. She couldn't think of another adjective. "You've done a lovely job with the house," she added.

"Thank you. Now, I know you two must be hungry. Let's go out onto the porch and we'll have our little lunch."

"Do you need some help?" Becky asked.

"No thank you," Mrs. Stearns said. "Annie can manage."

Becky blushed. Of course, she should have known. Mrs. Stearns did not look like the type to do her own cooking.

Tom pulled out a chair first for his mother and then for Becky, before seating himself between them at the small white wicker table. Becky carefully unfolded her napkin and took a sip of water from the crystal goblet. The screen door creaked as a large, matronly woman bustled out with a round platter which she first offered to Mrs. Stearns.

"Artichokes! My favorite!" Tom cried.

Mrs. Stearns smiled. "Since Becky has been so kind about helping us, I decided to have Annie make us something a little festive," she said. "I hope you like them, Becky, as much as Tom does."

"Oh, I do," Becky said, hoping that she sounded convincing. Why couldn't it be bologna sandwiches? Or grilled cheese? Or even Campbell's soup?

She watched Tom surreptitiously, to see how he ate them. They weren't so bad. They were sort of bland. The trick was in pulling off the leaves, dipping the ends in the dressing and then nibbling the small quantity of edible vegetable at the very end. Cutting the heart out of the prickly inside and eating it was somewhat more tricky but she managed to pull it off.

Mrs. Stearns chatted easily about Boston and River Bend. She asked Becky several casual questions about River Bend High and was extremely interested in Becky's answers.

She mentioned an art exhibit that was going to be in Chicago. "Several of Grandmother's Monets will be in the show," she explained to Becky. "Martin and I may drive up for it."

"Grandmother Remmington collected mostly Impressionist paintings," Tom told Becky.

Becky was scheduled to take an art appreciation course next fall in school. No way was she going to admit that she wasn't quite sure who Monet was. Becky smiled and nodded and pretended to understand as Mrs. Stearns discussed several of the paintings that Mrs. Remmington had owned.

Next, Mrs. Stearns talked about her favorite topic: Chinese porcelain. Becky was completely lost as Mrs. Stearns discussed Chinese dynasties, pottery glazes and ceremonial jars. Once again, Becky listened and smiled.

Becky decided that Edith Wharton might be a good topic of conversation to introduce, so she told Mrs. Stearns that she had just finished *The Age of Innocence* and had begun reading *The House of Mirth*, an earlier novel.

"Her view of society," Mrs. Stearns said, "is rather jaded I'm afraid and, of course, completely vindictive."

Becky didn't know what to say; she smiled.

Mrs. Stearns placed her knife and fork carefully in the center of her plate.

"Grandmother Remmington," she said, "despised her."

Becky was flabbergasted. "She knew Edith Wharton?"

"In Newport," Mrs. Stearns said. "And in Paris, of course."

That did it. Becky felt that she should just tuck

her tail between her legs and slink off to a corner. Instead, she carefully refolded her napkin and laid it beside her plate. She felt the lunch had been a disaster, as if she had failed somehow in front of Mrs. Stearns. Becky hadn't spilled her water or dropped her fork on the floor but she felt as though Mrs. Stearns had been secretly watching her, judging her reactions to the conversation and measuring Becky against a standard that Becky did not understand.

Becky glanced at Tom. He smiled at her. He was his usual, easygoing self and didn't seem to notice Becky's discomfort. Luckily, he suggested that they get back to work.

Becky was glad to get away from the luncheon table and get back to the work of methodically brushing the paint on the walls.

"Your great-grandmother sounds like an amazing lady," Becky said.

"I guess she was," Tom said. "She died before I was born. But Mom was very close to her."

Tom began to sing along with an old song that came on the radio. As Becky brushed the pale blue paint around one of the window frames and listened to Tom singing behind her, she made up her mind to change herself just as much as she could in order to fit more comfortably into Tom's world. She couldn't spend the rest of her life not knowing about artichokes and Monet and Chinese vases and the myriad of other things that Tom took so for granted.

She would start Saturday, she told herself with a firm resolve. She had the day off and she would, first, go shopping for some new clothes.

# 7

Hey, Marion," Todd called from outside Becky's room, "You up?" He pushed the door open and stuck his head in.

Becky was sitting up in bed.

"Mom's at work and Dad's playing tennis and I'm starving."

"You're always starving."

"I need nourishment," he said. "I am a growing boy."

Becky looked at him skeptically.

"C'mon," he pleaded, "let's fix a big breakfast."

Becky realized that she also was starving. "O.K.," she said as she got out of bed and pulled on a robe.

"What would you like?" she asked as she headed for the kitchen.

"What I'd like," Todd said, "is blueberry pancakes, fresh sausage, fried eggs, whole wheat toast, fresh orange juice . . ."

"How about scrambled eggs and bacon?"

"Cool."

"I'll start the bacon and you get the eggs ready."

"It's a deal."

Becky was busy frying the bacon when Todd, who was cracking eggs into a mixing bowl, said, "You really like him, huh?"

Becky spaced the sizzling bacon evenly in the pan with the fork she was holding and looked over at her baby brother. Except, in that instant, he didn't seem so much like a baby brother anymore. He was much taller than she was and even though he was wearing a faded Darth Vader T-shirt and gym shorts, he looked like a mature young man. Todd, without any warning, had switched into being an adult with her. She decided she had better answer his question honestly.

"Yes. I really do."

"He seems like a really neat guy," Todd said, stirring the eggs with a wooden spoon.

"He is," Becky said simply. "He's different from any guy I've ever met before."

"Hey," Todd said, "you think maybe I could go to the park with you sometime? To play with the dog or something?"

Todd had done the quick switch back. He was a kid again. "Yuck," Becky said. "Who wants a little brother tagging along?"

"Aw, c'mon. His Jeep looks so cool." Todd stopped stirring the eggs and looked at her, a gleam in his eye. "Say yes," he threatened, "or I'll pour runny, slimy eggs all down your back."

He picked up the mixing bowl and held it menacingly towards her.

"You wouldn't dare."

"Wouldn't I? Remember," he said, drawing himself up to his full height, "I'm bigger than you now." He tried to grab the collar of Becky's robe.

"Stop," Becky said, grinning. "I'm too hungry to waste the eggs. I can't promise anything but I will ask Tom if you can go with us sometime."

"Promise you'll ask?"

"Yes."

"Cool," Todd said, thrusting the mixing bowl at her. "You make the eggs and I'll start the toast."

In a few minutes they were both seated on the carpet in the family room, heaping plates of breakfast in front of them, laughing at Todd's favorite television show.

It was pretty silly but when Todd started giggling, Becky couldn't help herself, and she started giggling too.

"It's so dumb," Becky said, trying to stop smiling.

Todd was still laughing when the episode was over. "But it's so funny," he said.

Becky looked at the clock. "I've got to get ready," she said. "Laurie K.'s picking me up in a little while."

Todd offered to clean up the kitchen. That was a surprise.

"Thanks," Becky said, as she deposited her plate in the sink. "You know, you're not such a bad little brother after all."

"Yeah," Todd said, nodding his head up and down vigorously.

Becky stood up on tiptoe and kissed him quickly on the cheek. That embarrassed him. It also surprised Becky. She dashed out of the kitchen and headed for her room.

"Thanks for making breakfast," Todd yelled.

Becky dashed in and out of the shower, dressed and made sure she had the money from her paycheck tucked safely inside her purse.

She heard Laurie K.'s car honk from the driveway and ran out and hopped in the front seat. Laurie K. zipped the car out of the subdivision and headed for the highway.

She and Jeff were back together she reported. Their date last night had been incredible. They had gone to the Cardinals' baseball game in St. Louis—they won—and then gone out for hamburgers. Jeff had held her hand and said he loved her and there had been moonlight and, well, everything . . .

Becky wondered what exactly "and, well, everything . . ." meant but before she could ask, Laurie K. had gone on to a new topic.

"I got a postcard from Jonathan. It's a picture of the Student Union at U. of I. He said he was busy and just about to start with a new group of kids." Laurie K. successfully navigated the turn onto the highway. "He sounds like he misses River Bend. And he said to tell you hello."

"Tell him I said hi."

"Why don't you write him a letter?"

"Why don't you?"

"I'm going to," Laurie K. said, speeding up to pass a little old lady in a Buick. "You're making a mistake there. He's such a neat guy."

"I know he's a neat guy," Becky replied. "But I've got Tom now. Remember?"

"How could I forget? Boy, is he a hunk. But it

wouldn't hurt to be nice to Jonathan . . . just in case."

"Just in case of what?"

"I don't know," Laurie K. said. She glanced into the rear-view mirror and changed into the right-hand lane. "In case something happens between you and Tom."

"What could happen?"

"I don't know. A thousand things," she said, turning into the parking lot for the shopping mall.

"Nothing's going to happen," Becky said. They walked toward the entrance to the mall.

Laurie K. wanted to look for a new pair of jeans but she had really come along to keep Becky company. Becky knew exactly where she wanted to go and led the way into the Campus Shop at one of the big department stores.

"What are we doing in here?" Laurie K. asked, looking around at all the traditional, preppy clothes.

"I want to get a couple of shirts," Becky said, stopping by a display of button-down, Oxford cloth shirts.

"But it's all so boring," Laurie K. said. "This isn't your style at all."

"I'm going to try something different."

"And give up all those frilly blouses that you look so good in?"

"Can I help you?"

Becky turned to the young saleswoman who was smiling at her. The thing that Becky noticed was her hair. It was about the same length as Becky's but instead of being parted in the middle, it was parted on the side, pulled across the top of her head, and then secured with a gold barrette. Becky realized that it was the classic style for preppy girls. She filed the information away to use later.

"I'd like to get a couple of shirts," she said. "A white one and a blue one, please."

The young woman helped her find her size and the color she was looking for.

"Boring," Laurie K. intoned, when Becky came out of the dressing room with the white shirt on. "Ve-ry bor-ing."

Becky looked at herself in the mirror. It was a change. But it fit well. "My wardrobe needs a few classic pieces of clothing," she said, in self-defense. "I'm going to take them."

Laurie K. approved of Becky's next purchases which were a pale yellow crew-neck sweater and a plain navy blue skirt. But she threatened to abandon Becky at the mall and end their friendship when Becky tried on a murky-colored, wrap-around Madras skirt.

"That is the ugliest skirt I've ever seen," she hissed.

Becky smiled sheepishly at her. "You're right."

Next, on Becky's list was a new pair of penny loafers. In the shoe department, she tried on a pair of wine-colored ones.

Laurie K. flopped down in one of the chairs. "What is all this?" she demanded. "Are you going preppy on me?"

Becky didn't answer. She was studying the shoes in the mirror.

"You are, aren't you?"

"What's wrong with it?"

"Nothing's wrong with it," Laurie K. answered. "It just doesn't seem like you." She pointed to a pair of finely crafted yellow sandals with low heels. "Those seem more like you."

Becky looked at the sandals. They didn't fit at all with the new Becky that was about to emerge.

"Next," Laurie K. said, screwing up her face, "you'll be talking in a Bah-ston accent and saying 'Mummy and Daddy'."

"My dear, dear friend Laurie," Becky said, trying to imitate a Boston accent, "Thomas and I will always send you a Christmas card from Massachusetts."

"Barf!"

The loafers were a lot more expensive than Becky had thought they would be, but she decided to buy them anyway.

Back in the mall, Laurie K. decided to go in and look for a pair of jeans. She found a pair of violet-colored jean-style pants that fit her perfectly. They also came in a light green color and she tried to talk Becky into getting a pair.

"No," Becky said, "I don't really need another pair of slacks. But I think I'll try these on."

*"Those?"* Laurie K. said incredulously, looking at the khaki bermuda shorts that Becky had pulled off the rack.

"They're very in," Becky said. The bermudas were double pleated and had cuffs around the bottoms.

"They look like something a camp fire girl would wear."

Becky put on the shorts and came out of the dressing room.

"They're so baggy."

"They're supposed to be loose-fitting," Becky said crossly. "They'll look terrific with one of my new shirts and my new shoes."

"Don't you think you're carrying this a little

too far? Let's get out of here before you buy something really disgusting."

Becky purchased the bermudas and they piled all the bags in the backseat of the car. Laurie K. was silent most of the way home. "You know," she said finally, "he's not going to like you better because of the way you dress."

"I know that," she said. "I just think it's time to try something new."

Laurie K. fiddled with the radio buttons until she found a song she liked. "You're not going overboard, are you?"

"No."

"Tom's a real fox," Laurie K. said, "but he is different from us."

"What do you mean?"

"People from the East Coast are just different than people from Illinois."

"But that's one of the things that I like about him." Laurie K. was a real dyed-in-the-wool Midwesterner. She liked River Bend and she liked Illinois and she had a tendency to be suspicious of people whose backgrounds were different from hers.

"Mrs. Stearns comes into the store a lot," Laurie K. said. "She's pleasant and all but I always get the feeling that she thinks of us as . . . shopkeepers."

Becky didn't know what to say. The Kaynors were one of the oldest families in town. The store had been in business for almost fifty years. "She's just more reserved than people around here," Becky said lamely.

Becky felt uncomfortable. She wanted Laurie K. to be supportive of the new image that she was going to try and project. But at the same time, how could she defend Mrs. Stearns if Mrs. Stearns patronized her best friend?

"I almost forgot," Laurie K. said. "Jeff and I are going to the VFW Fun Days tonight. Why don't you and Tom come with us?"

Obviously, Laurie K. had had enough serious discussion.

"We're going to a play tonight."

"What?"

*"The Cherry Orchard."*

"What's that? A musical?"

"It's a Russian play," Becky explained, "about a family."

"Barf."

"It's at Abercrombie. Tom's already got the tickets."

The VFW Fun Days event was held at the park every summer in order to raise money for the city's Little League teams. Becky had been going for as long as she could remember but she thought it was probably more of an injection of small town life than Tom could handle.

"You sure are doing a lot of highbrow stuff."

"It's fun to do something different once in a while."

"I'll take Fun Days." Laurie K. turned off the highway and into the town of River Bend.

"I need to stop at the library," Becky said.

"Don't you get enough of that place during the week?"

"I just want to pick up a couple of things."

"I'll have to drop you off," Laurie K. said. "I promised Mom I'd help her with the night deposit at the store."

"That's O.K.," Becky said, as Laurie K. turned the car toward the library.

Becky climbed out of the car. "Thanks for driving to the Mall."

"Call me if you change your mind about tonight," Laurie K. said as she pulled the car away from the curb.

Becky waved to Mrs. Francis who was behind the front desk and headed straight for the record collection. She set her parcels down on a table and started to thumb through the albums. She was surprised, and a little dismayed, to see how many operas there were. And there were so many different people singing all the different operas. She found a Pavarotti version of *Tosca* but after that, she had no idea which ones to listen to.

As she was puzzling over all the different choices, Mr. Jones walked by. He smiled at Becky and came over to her.

"Good afternoon," he said. "I thought you were off today."

"I am," Becky answered, "but I just stopped by to pick up some music."

"Opera?" Mr. Jones said, raising one eyebrow.

Becky nodded. "I think it's time I learned more about it. But I don't even know where to start."

"Well," he said, moving closer to the record bin, "the one you've got is a good place to begin. It's a bit ponderous in the middle, but the ending is a pip."

Becky smiled at him. "I know," she said, "I heard it a couple of days ago."

"It's quite different from what you listen to nowadays, I daresay." His eyes were twinkling at her.

Becky felt that special warmth for him that she had felt ever since the day he had helped her with her meeting with Tom. "Now, let's see," he continued. "I would suggest starting easy. With, perhaps, some of the more famous operas." He pulled out a recording. "Here we are. Mozart is always nice. Try *The Magic Flute,* and, let's see, yes, *La Bohème.*"

He handed the records to Becky. They weighed a ton. "Those should keep you busy for a while," he said, smiling at her. "I don't suppose a certain young man is also interested in opera?"

"He is," she admitted. "Kind of. And I thought it wouldn't hurt, you know . . ."

"No," he said, kindly, "it never hurts. But do go easy. Opera is an acquired taste."

Becky thanked him and watched him walk back to the Periodicals department.

Should she get a book on Chinese porcelain? Was that going too far? She wanted Mrs. Stearns to like her, to approve of her, and maybe being able to talk about Mrs. Stearns's hobby would be a way to break the ice. She found a large picture book with hundreds of color illustrations. Yes, she would check it out too.

She found Mrs. Francis and discovered that the book on John Singer Sargent that she had asked to borrow from another library that traded books with the River Bend library had arrived.

Miss Stevenson checked the book and the records out for Becky. "Are you working on a special project?" she asked.

"In a way," Becky responded, smiling.

The books, the records and her new clothes weighed about three tons and even though it was just a short walk, Becky was really glad to get home. Her father was in the kitchen preparing supper.

"Look at you," he said, "did you buy out the stores?"

"Just a few things," Becky said, putting up her cheek for his kiss. "And I stopped by the library for some books and things."

"Dinner's not for awhile," he informed her, "do you want something to eat?"

"No thanks," Becky called, as she headed for her room.

She dumped everything gratefully into the middle of her bed. Her arms felt as though they were going to fall off. She massaged her forearm and decided she would start at the beginning of *Tosca*. Becky pulled the first album out of the case and put it on her stereo. She closed her door and started unpacking her new clothes. The next best thing to buying new clothes and wearing them, was trying them on just as soon as you got home.

Becky took her new pale blue shirt out of the package and slipped into it. Then she put on the navy skirt and her new penny loafers. She looked at herself in the mirror. "Maybe Laurie K.'s right," she said out loud to the strange person she saw in the reflection. "It is a little boring."

She rolled up the sleeves of the shirt twice. Better. Then she got out the new sweater and draped it casually over her shoulders and tied the sleeves together in front. Better still. Now, jewelry. Opening her jewelry box, she surveyed the collection of chains, necklaces, and earrings inside. Becky had some nice pieces of jewelry since her mother got a discount on everything at the store.

She selected a plain gold bangle bracelet and slipped it on her left wrist. And her pearls for her neck. Finally, she clipped on a pair of single pearl earrings. Once again, she looked at herself in the mirror. The jewelry helped enormously.

But her hair? She remembered the way the girl in the store had worn hers. Quickly, Becky parted her hair on the side, pulled it over to the other side and, finding a barrette in her vanity drawer, secured it. She brushed her bangs toward the side too.

Back in front of the full length mirror, Becky was surprised by the totally different looking person who was looking back at her. She looked very sophisticated and tailored, as though ready to step onto a private sailboat for a lazy ride down the . . . what was the name of that river in Boston? The Charles, that was it. She looked as though she were ready for a lazy trip down the Charles, or maybe an afternoon of socializing at the country club.

Then a doubt snaked into her mind. Was it too much of a change? Would Tom notice? If he did notice, would he think it was too studied? No, she decided, again pleased with her image, she would mix her new purchases in with her old slacks and skirts, and besides, Tom was used to lots of girls who dressed like this so he would undoubtedly take it for granted. But she hoped, secretly, that he would notice.

The music intruded on Becky's thoughts. A high female voice was singing a long aria. Somehow, the music didn't sound as good now as it did with Tom in the Jeep. In fact, it sounded kind of piercing and boring. Well, as Mr. Jones said, it was an acquired taste.

There was a knock on her door and Todd stuck his head inside. "What's that awful noise?"

"Todd," Becky said sharply, "you're supposed to wait for me to say, 'Come in'."

"I thought maybe you'd died or something. What is that anyway?"

"It's opera."

"You mean a fat lady dressed in a Viking costume?"

"No," Becky said, exasperated. "It's *Tosca.*"

"Well you can have *Tosca,*" he said. "But don't ask me to listen to it!" He started whistling as loud as he could.

"Buzz off, will you."

"What'd you do to yourself?"

Becky was about ready to strangle him. He could be such a pain sometimes. "I didn't do anything. I just bought some new clothes. Now leave me alone."

"You look like a den mother."

"Arrrr," Becky growled and started toward him.

"O.K. O.K.," he said, backing out the door. "Dad told me to tell you that dinner's in five minutes. It's meatloaf." He was almost out the door. "And you know the best thing about meatloaf . . ."

Becky slammed the door in his face.

Todd opened the door quickly and said, "The best thing about meatloaf is cold meatloaf sandwiches." He closed the door.

Becky reached over and locked it.

Todd rattled the doorknob. "With ketchup," he yelled from the other side.

"Toad, I am going to kill you one of these days," Becky said to the closed door.

She walked over and turned up the volume on the stereo. He was just impossible sometimes. Becky couldn't stand the shrieking soprano voice that filled the room, so she turned the volume back down.

Looking at herself in the mirror again, Becky decided that she really did like her new look and she liked her hair parted on the side. She changed back into her regular clothes and began to put her new purchases away. As she listened to the opera music, she wondered what the Stearns were having for dinner. Were they getting ready to sit down to some elegant gourmet meal?

The Johnsons' Saturday night supper was what her father called The Ultimate American Meal, or the UAM. It consisted of meatloaf, mashed potatoes, corn and for dessert, chocolate pudding. It was one of Becky's favorite meals. And Todd was right. There was nothing better than cold meatloaf sandwiches—with ketchup.

Becky took the recording off the stereo. She would have to take her opera lessons in small doses. Maybe she would try *The Magic Flute* tomorrow.

## 8

Becky put the recording of *The Magic Flute* on her stereo. She liked *The Magic Flute* better than she did *Tosca*. The music was more melodic and the singer's voices didn't seem as harsh. She had checked a book titled *101 Stories of Famous Operas* out of the library. She had read the biographical sketches of Mozart and Puccini and looked over the librettos for the operas. The more she knew about the composers and the stories of the operas, the easier it was to appreciate them. But she was a long way, however, from being an opera buff. It seemed, at times, a real chore to force herself to listen to the music and to read the books about it.

Becky had read the book on John Singer Sargent. Since she enjoyed biographies, she had found it interesting. Toward the end of the book on Sargent, there had been a full-page, color reproduction of the portrait of Mrs. Remmington. "Cecilia Thorndike Remmington. Painted, 1910. Private Collection," the caption had read. It was the first time Becky had ever known anyone who owned a museum-quality painting and it made her even a little more in awe of the Stearns and Mrs. Stearns in particular.

She looked at herself in the wide mirror above the bathroom sink. Tom had complimented her on her new clothes and told her how much he liked her new hair style. But was she carrying it too far? she asked her reflection. Was she trying too hard to be something that she was not? Becky Johnson, she told herself, just wanted to fit a little more smoothly into the world of Tom Stearns. But what exactly was that world? Wasn't it River Bend now that he had moved to Illinois? Was she a part of his world now?

Becky wondered if Tom's self-assurance and his easy confidence came from the fact that he had been born to a family with a social background and inherited wealth. Unlike herself, who didn't quite know where she was going—or even, at times, who she really was—Tom seemed to have an inbred assurance that everything would turn out terrifically for him.

Was it his parents' money that gave him that advantage? The Stearns didn't have to worry about house payments and car payments and how they were going to pay for their children's college educations. Was that what gave them the freedom to care about things like Chinese pottery and real antiques?

Becky started brushing her hair. Were people

just automatically supposed to care about the arts? And culture? Maybe, she reasoned, those things were intrinsically important no matter how much money you had.

She loved the feeling of information, of knowledge that sometimes almost overwhelmed her at the library. It was as if all the great ideas and the achievements of mankind were right there on the bookshelves. Yet, she had always looked on her passion for reading and her love of books as more of a pastime. It was just something she did, the way that L.W. consumed magazines or Laurie K. followed the Cardinals.

She smiled at herself in the mirror. The new Becky Johnson had been a big hit the night of the play. Although the play had been interminable and even Tom had agreed that Chekhov had probably lost something in the translation from the Russian.

The phone rang. Becky started to go out into the hall to answer it but it stopped in the middle of the second ring.

"TELEPHONE," Todd yelled, from all the way back in the family room.

Becky put down her hair brush and went out and picked up the phone.

"Have you recovered from *The Cherry Orchard?*" Tom asked.

His voice sent a little thrill of excitement down Becky's spine.

"I think so," Becky said. "How about you?"

"I took a shower and gargled," Tom said, "that seemed to help."

"I thought you had class today," Becky said.

"It's been canceled. I'm free all day."

110

Becky sat down on the carpet and lazily twined the phone cord around her finger.

"Would you like to do something today?" he asked.

"I don't really have any plans," Becky responded. That wasn't the whole truth. She had talked to L.W. about possibly going to the pool.

"It's supposed to be a real scorcher of a day," Tom informed her. "The forecast is for the temperature to hit a hundred degrees."

"Welcome to Illinois," Becky said.

"That's what my father keeps saying."

"It's good for the corn."

"It's growing so hard it's keeping me awake at night!"

Becky laughed. They both knew that the nearest cornfield was at least half a mile from his house.

Would Tom like to go to the pool? Here she was, making an all-out effort to learn more about his world without even trying to show him more of her own. Besides, the only kids he had met were L.W. and Laurie K.

"Let's go to the pool."

"Great," Tom said. "That's just what I was going to suggest."

"What time shall I pick you up?"

"How about one o'clock? Oh," she said, remembering Todd's earlier request, "would you mind taking Todd along? He's dying for a ride in the Jeep."

"Not at all. See you at one."

Becky hung up the phone and went into her room to get dressed. She pulled on a pair of shorts and slipped into a tank top. She quickly made her bed and cleaned up her room. She gathered up her dirty laundry and dropped it down the clothes chute in the hallway on her way to the kitchen.

Todd was in the family room, lying on his stomach on the floor, watching a game show on television. The kitchen and the family room were a mess. Becky could never understand how one fourteen-year-old could completely clutter up two whole rooms in the space of a single morning.

"This place looks like a pigsty."

"Shhhh," Todd prompted her. "This guy's just about to go for the big prize."

Becky sat down on the footstool in the family room. They both watched breathlessly as the contestant was put through his paces. He blew it.

Becky stood up. "It is time, Toad," she said, "for you to pick up some of this junk. I bet you haven't made your bed and it's your week to mow the yard."

Todd rolled over on the carpeting and pulled a pillow over his face. "Awww, Marion," he mumbled, "leave me alone."

"That," Becky said, "was Tom on the telephone and we're going to the pool this afternoon."

"Big deal."

Becky prodded Todd's leg with her toe. "If you want a ride to the pool in you-know-whose really *cool* you-know-what, you better get some of these chores done."

Todd jerked the pillow away from his face with both hands. "Yeah?"

"Yeah," Becky said as she started for the kitchen.

Todd jumped up from the floor and in a couple

of minutes stumbled through the kitchen, his arms loaded down with all his junk.

Becky started putting the dirty breakfast dishes in the dishwasher. Her parents believed in democracy about household chores—where she and Todd were concerned, that is. In the summer, they had to take turns, week by week, either mowing the yard or tidying up the house in the mornings. Especially since her mother had gone back to work. And they also had to help with the dinner dishes in the evening. It just happened that it was Becky's week to work inside.

She was just finishing with the dishes when Todd dashed out the door. She heard the mower start up outside. There was nothing like the right incentive to help get Todd moving, Becky thought.

Todd and Becky had a quick sandwich at noon and watched television as they waited for Tom to arrive. Tom knocked on the family room door exactly on the stroke of one. Todd jumped up and let him in.

"Hi, Todd. How you doing?"

"Pretty good."

"I brought this for you," Tom said, holding out a white bicyclist cap.

"Wow!" Todd grabbed the hat and yanked it down on his head. "How does it look?"

"Cool," Tom said. "But you're supposed to wear the bill turned up." He reached out and adjusted the front of the cap. "Like this."

Todd leaned over and looked at his reflection in the glass of one of the pictures on the wall. "Thanks," he said, turning his head to the left and to the right.

"Hello," Becky said. "Remember me?"

Tom flashed her a wide, gorgeous grin. "Oh hi, Becky. Are you going to the pool too?"

Becky picked up her pool bag by its shoulder strap and swung it at Tom. He ducked, laughing at her.

Becky would have liked to give Tom a little hello kiss but she knew she couldn't in front of Todd.

"Are we going to the pool or not?" Todd asked impatiently.

Tom held the door open wide. "After you."

Becky and Todd preceded him out to the Jeep which was parked in the driveway.

"Where's Maxwell?" Todd asked.

"Maxwell is home by the air-conditioner," Tom said. "Where all good Irish Setters should be on a day like this."

Todd climbed into the back and Becky got into the passenger side. Tom put on his sunglasses and started the engine.

Todd put one elbow on the back of each seat and leaned between the middle space. "Do you really like all the opera stuff?" he asked.

"Why?"

"Becky's been driving us nuts listening to it."

Becky had told Tom that she was listening to a few operas and they had discussed *The Magic Flute,* but she could have killed Todd for bringing up the topic like that.

Tom laughed. "My brother's a musician," he explained to Todd, "and my mother likes opera so it's always been around. Don't you like it?"

"Naw," Todd said, "all that screeching and foreign language and stuff."

"You have no appreciation of music," Becky

said, only half joking. She reached over and pulled the bill of the cap down over Todd's eyes.

"Watch it, Marion," Todd warned, as he readjusted the cap.

Becky turned on the radio thinking that maybe that would shut Todd up. A popular rock and roll song blared out at them.

"Now that's more like it," Todd said. "Hey, how fast will this thing go?"

Tom turned a corner. "Not really fast," he said. "It's more for rough terrain than it is for speed."

Todd monopolized the conversation all the way to the pool. Becky would have liked to talk to Tom a little more about opera or maybe about the book on Chinese porcelain but she could barely get a word into the conversation. And, besides, she knew it would be impossible to have a serious discussion with the talkative Toad in the back seat.

"I almost forgot," Tom said, during a lull in Todd's chatter. "Edge is coming to visit. Remember? My friend from Boston."

"The guy you used to go sailing with?"

"He's on his way to California," Tom explained, "and he's going to stay here for a week."

"When does he arrive?"

"Next week. I'm looking forward to his visit."

Becky tried to remember the friend's real name. Edgington? Was that it? Tom had talked about him a lot when they first met but lately he hadn't mentioned him as often.

"I really want you to meet him," Tom said. "I think you'll like him."

"There's Jake," Todd yelled as they turned into the pool parking lot. Jake was standing by the entrance waiting for him. Todd stood up and waved his arms back and forth. "Jake," he screamed. "Hey, Jake." Todd was acting like a big shot because he was arriving in Tom's Jeep.

Jake came trotting over to meet them and they all went inside.

"C'mon, Tom," Todd said in a proprietary tone, "I'll show you where to put your clothes." He led Tom off to the locker room.

Becky already had her suit on under her outfit so she put her clothes into a basket in the girl's locker room and went outside to wait for Tom.

He came out in a couple of minutes. Becky watched him as he walked toward her. He looked terrific. Tall and lean and muscular. Her heart swelled with pride that he was her boyfriend. She was excited, and a trifle anxious, about introducing him to the other kids.

"Here we go," Tom said, touching her hand lightly.

He was a bit nervous, too, Becky realized, and that made her feel stronger and more confident. She led the way to the section of the pool where the kids always hung out.

"Hi, Tom," L.W. greeted him, looking up from her magazine.

"Hello," he responded. "How's the Japanese coming?"

Tom had helped L.W. find a Japanese student at Abercrombie who was willing to tutor her. She had begun her private lessons two weeks ago. L.W. had decided to become fluent in Japanese, get her master's degree in business and become the first female president of IBM.

"Slowly," L.W. said. "Very slowly."

Tom turned to Laurie K. "Hello," he said.

"You should see the paint in my room. It looks great."

Becky was proud of Tom. He seemed at ease and was making an effort to be friendly.

Laurie K. introduced him to Jeff.

They shook hands. Becky watched them as they carefully sized each other up. Tom was taller than Jeff but Jeff was heavier. Becky wondered why boys always had to do that? Then she realized that girls always looked each other over too—they were just more subtle about it.

Becky introduced him to Mary, Debbie and Monica, to Len, Cliff and Mark. Tom was relaxed and cordial. He smiled and repeated people's names in order to remember them, just the way you're supposed to.

They found two empty chairs and threw their towels over them.

"Let's get in the pool," Tom said.

"You go ahead," Becky said, lowering herself into her chair. "I want to sit in the sun for awhile."

Tom walked to the edge of the pool and did a low, racer's dive into the water. In what seemed like about two seconds to Becky, he was on the opposite side of the pool. He executed an underwater swimmer's turn on the wall of the pool and swam lazily back toward her.

Wasn't there anything that he didn't do well?

L.W., sitting in the shade as usual, raised her sunglasses onto her forehead. "He is a real hunk," she whispered.

Becky already knew that but it was always nice to hear someone else say it too.

Tom climbed out of the pool and came over and

settled in the chair next to Becky. He mixed easily into the conversation. He didn't know many of the people or events that the kids talked about but he was interested and followed the gossip and the chatter easily. Becky was afraid that he might overcompensate for feeling out of place by talking too much about Boston or rugby or sailing but he only mentioned those when somebody asked him a direct question and he appeared to be having a good time.

Then Jeff raised himself up off his towel and said, "Hey, Tom, what'd you think of the Cardinals' game against Montreal?"

"I didn't see it," Tom replied.

"You didn't see it!" Jeff glanced at Laurie K. "Man, I couldn't believe it when those guys both got home runs in the sixth."

"I bet that was great," Tom said.

"Did you see the game the next night?" Jeff demanded.

Tom shook his head.

"It wasn't as good," Jeff said, "but could you believe that game against Pittsburgh? I mean, seventeen innings!"

Tom smiled at him. "You're kidding? Seventeen innings?"

"Didn't you see that one either?" Jeff asked.

Tom admitted that he hadn't.

"Hey, Becky," Jeff said, "what's the matter with this guy? Doesn't he like baseball?"

Becky didn't know what to say. She and Tom had never talked about baseball. Since River Bend was so close to St. Louis, everybody in town was a Cardinal fan. "Tom just moved here," she said feebly. "Remember."

"I don't know," Jeff said, shaking his head

sadly from side to side, as if to suggest that there was something terribly wrong with a guy who didn't know about the Cardinals.

Becky had no idea as to how to try and save the situation.

"I used to follow the Red Sox," Tom said, referring to the Boston team, "but since I moved, I've sort of been in-between."

Jeff stood up and stretched and flexed his muscles. "You better get with it," he said. "This is Cardinal territory around here." He stalked off to the diving board.

The other kids slowly resumed their conversations. Becky was annoyed. Why did Jeff have to pull a number like that?

"I'm sorry," she whispered to Tom. "Jeff can be a pain sometimes."

"It's O.K.," he said softly. "I like baseball. I just haven't paid much attention to it recently."

Becky reached over and laid her hand on his. He opened his palm and entwined his fingers through hers.

Jeff was showing off on the diving board, strutting around as if he owned the pool and joking with some of the younger guys who idolized him. Everybody watched as he pranced around and did several mediocre dives off the board. His dives were energetic and they made a lot of splashes but that was about all that could be said for them.

Finally, he came over and laid down on a towel next to Laurie K. He looked immensely pleased with himself.

Tom leaned over and put his mouth close to Becky's ear. "Do you want me to show off a little?"

"What do you mean?" she whispered back.

"I'm a pretty good diver."

"What are you two whispering about?" L.W. asked in a conspiratorial tone. "Jeff?"

"I thought I'd try the diving board," Tom said, standing up.

Tom walked over and got in line. When his turn came, he stepped nimbly out to the end of the board and did two experimental jumps, testing the spring and the tension of the board. He walked back to the head of the board and paused for a few seconds, concentrating. Then he took three steps, a firm leap, and executed a perfect one-and-a-half front flip into the pool. His body sliced into the water and just barely caused a ripple on the surface.

He smiled at Becky as he hoisted himself out of the pool. "This one," he said, raising his voice just enough so that Jeff could hear, "is going to be a front flip with a laid-back half twist."

He performed the second dive as if he were an Olympic athlete competing in the Summer Games. Becky, had she been a judge, would have given him a perfect score of ten.

Becky was amazed. Where had Tom learned to dive like that? She watched him as he climbed the ladder to the high board. He was so tall and athletic and good looking. Becky was still astounded at times by the fact that he liked her.

Tom was balanced carefully on the end of the board, ready to do a back dive. With a powerful push from his toes, he soared out into the air. His tanned body glistened and his red trunks stood out against the blue sky as he did a graceful one and a half back flip. His tuck was perfect and with his arms extended above his head and his toes pointed upward, once again, he barely rippled the water.

The kids were beginning to comment on Tom's diving. Becky glanced over at Jeff. He was pretending to be uninterested but she could tell that he was watching every move that Tom made.

Tom climbed to the high board once again and performed a double flip into the water. He swam lazily over to the edge and climbed out.

Becky saw Jeff lay back down on his towel and close his eyes. Laurie K. said something to him but Becky couldn't hear her.

Becky was so proud of Tom that her heart was about to burst. Things were even now between Jeff and Tom, and Becky hoped they would stay that way.

Todd came charging up to Tom. "What cool diving!" he almost shouted.

"Thanks," Tom said. He paused to shake the water out of his hair.

Todd followed him as Tom came over and sat down next to Becky.

"Where did you learn to dive like that?" L.W. asked.

"I spent a few summers at camp," Tom said casually, "and I just picked it up."

"Were you on the diving team at school?" Todd asked.

"No," he responded, "the school didn't have a diving team."

Jake yelled for Todd to rejoin him at the other end of the pool. Todd went galloping off.

Tom leaned toward L.W. "Do you want the truth?" he asked her, keeping his voice low.

He knew exactly how to talk to L.W. She

always wanted the truth. But was he going to say something about Jeff? Becky steeled herself for Tom's next statement.

"Of course," L.W. said, intrigued.

"Diving scares me to death," Tom said, his eyes looking serious. "I only do it to prove to myself that I can."

Becky was shocked. After that incredible display and Tom was admitting that he had been petrified the whole time. Becky respected him more for his admission of fear than she did for his diving. Both took real courage.

"Don't you have something that you do like that?" Tom asked L.W.

L.W. chewed on her thumb thoughtfully. "No," she said. "I always just do things because they need to be done."

"Pretty good diving," Jeff said, suddenly looming above them.

"Thanks," Tom said easily.

Becky held her breath. Was Jeff going to pick a fight?

"My swan dives are lousy. You think you could show me how to do one?"

Tom squinted his eyes against the sun. "Sure," he said. "C'mon."

Becky let out her breath.

Tom got up to follow Jeff to the diving board.

L.W. let out a heavy sigh as she and Becky watched Tom walk away. "Do you think there are any more out there like him?"

"I doubt it," Becky said.

## 9

**R**obots," Sean said, looking up at Becky from the other side of the library's front desk.

"Robots," Becky repeated thoughtfully. "I think we might have something on them. Let's go see what we can find." Sean scurried ahead of her and into the Children's department. His mother was allowing him to come to the library on his own now. Becky walked over to the science section and pulled a book off the shelf. "Here's *The Star Wars Book About Robots*," she said, handing it to him.

"Artoo!" Sean cried, seeing the illustration of the droid on the cover.

Becky smiled at him. "R2-D2 and C-3PO are your guides in the book," she explained. "Through the fascinating world of robots."

Sean was listening to her carefully.

"The other books on robots are right here," Becky told him, indicating several titles on the shelf. "After you look at that one, take a look at these too." It was better, after all, for him to do a little exploring on his own. "I'll be behind the desk if you need any more help."

"Thanks," he said, moving over to look at the other titles.

"You're welcome." She reached out and ruffled his blond hair with her hand.

Becky walked back to the desk feeling really good about her job. Sean had become one of the high points of the summer. When he had finished with rockets, Becky had suggested airplanes, then trains. Robots should keep him busy for about a week. But then what could she suggest? Outer space? Computers? Sean was only eight years old but he was a very bright eight-year-old. Wouldn't it be neat, she thought, if he became a famous engineer or an inventor. Maybe she would try and interest him in some of the books on famous inventors—after robots and computers.

The library was busy for the next few minutes. First, there was a woman who needed information on Eugene O'Neill, the American playwright. Becky helped her find two books of criticism and showed her the Drama section. Next, a college guy needed some books on how to apply for grants and scholarships. Becky took him to the Reference section and showed the books that might be of some help.

Just as Becky was about to take a breather, a slim, ethereal-looking young woman approached her.

"I need some books on Mexico," the woman said in a soft voice.

"Travel books?"

"No."

"Picture books?"

The woman shook her head.

"Novels?"

"I want to absorb the feel, the color, the romance of Mexico," she said, waving her hands delicately in the air, "although it could be South America."

Becky was puzzled. "I don't think I understand what you need."

"I want to set my dreams to dance," the woman said, swaying her torso back and forth. "I've been dreaming of Mexico and I want to choreograph my dreams."

Becky looked at her closely. Was she a weirdo? She did look like a dancer. Perhaps she was a dancer-choreographer.

"There are a couple of novels about the Aztecs," Becky told her, remembering two books that Miss Stevenson had read and liked recently. "Or maybe you should read Marquez—the South American writer who won the Nobel Prize."

"Yes," the woman said vaguely.

"Let me show you the card catalog," Becky said. "You can look under the subject index and then decide which titles look interesting." Becky led her to the card catalog cabinet, pulled out the drawer on Mexico, gave the woman a pencil and piece of paper and fled to the back of the library. Sometimes, the only thing to do with the strange ones was to show them where they should look and then go hide from them. Becky didn't do it very often but this dream dancer was clearly one of those cases.

Becky found herself in the gardening section.

Unconsciously, she rearranged three books that were out of alphabetical order. She remembered the aphids lady. The aphids lady had not been back to the library since her first visit so Becky assumed that she and her begonias were living in a blissful, aphid-free world now.

Remembering that day, Becky automatically thought of Tom. How excited and anxious she had been when they first started dating; and how wonderful the past month had been. Could this be the same Becky Johnson who had nervously typed title cards as she waited for a good-looking guy to come in and pick up his books on science?

Her appearance had changed so much. Today, she was dressed in her white button-down shirt, blue skirt, pearls and penny loafers. And her hair was pulled over to one side and held in place with a new gold barrette. Catching sight of herself in the glass of a framed print that was hanging on the wall, she was convinced that she could pass for a quiet, East Coast sophisticate any day. Becky Johnson had also changed on the inside. Now she knew about the two painters, Monet and Sargent, she could talk a little bit about opera and she was familiar with eighteenth century Imperial Chinese pottery. She grinned at her reflection. What she would ever do with the information on pottery, she wasn't quite sure—besides talk to Mrs. Stearns—but she had enjoyed reading the book.

Becky shook her light brown hair around her shoulders. She was ready for just about anything. And it was Tom Stearns who had helped bring about the transformation. Tom. She sighed. She hadn't seen him for the past three days. Not since Edge had arrived. He had called her yesterday to apologize and explain how busy he and Edge had been. Well, Becky thought, Edge was only staying a week and then she would have Tom back. She was disappointed about not seeing Tom and a little disappointed about not meeting Edge yet but she realized that he and Tom probably had a lot of catching up to do.

A part of Becky wanted to meet Malcolm Edgington Simpson III and the other part of her was apprehensive about it. The front doors to the library swooshed open. Becky automatically glanced up. It was Tom! And another guy. Was it Edge? It had to be.

In the flesh. He was shorter than Tom and had shaggy light brown hair. He had dark brown eyes, a long, thin nose, and a prominent chin. He was O.K. looking, Becky decided, but not nearly as handsome as Tom.

Had they come to see her? Or did Tom need a book? She felt a tremor of anxiety.

Edge pulled a pair of brown, horn-rimmed glasses out of his shirt pocket, put them on, surveyed the library and then replaced them in his pocket.

"There you are," Tom said, seeing Becky. The two guys walked across the floor toward her.

"Hi," Tom said, coming up to her. "Becky, this is Edge. Becky Johnson, Edge Simpson."

"Becky," Edge cried. "Hello, hello." He shook her hand enthusiastically. "All I've heard for the past three days is Becky, Becky, Becky."

Becky almost blushed. "I've heard a lot about you too."

"What a nice little library."

"Thank you."

"I must tell Father about this," Edge said.

"Is he interested in libraries?"

"Terribly," Edge said. "Harvard. Grandfather gave a building, and a collection and something else," he flapped one hand in the air, "I can never remember quite what. And Father keeps an eye on it."

Tom was smiling at them. Becky realized how much Edge, as his best friend, meant to him. The same way that L.W. and Laurie K. were so important to her.

"I hope you're free tonight . . ." Tom began.

"I just happened," Edge interrupted, "to be talking to a friend of my grandmother's in St. Louis and she gave me tickets to a Beethoven concert. For tonight. Now, I know it's dreadfully short notice but we thought perhaps you and your friend L . . . ?"

"L.W.," Tom supplied.

"That you and L.W. might go with us."

"Do you think she can make it?" Tom asked. Then he looked rather sheepish and ran his hand through the side of his hair. "I hope you can make it too," he added.

"That sounds like fun," Becky said. "Why don't I call L.W. and ask her?"

"Super," Edge said.

"The concert is outdoors," Tom explained. "In St. Louis. I thought we'd leave at six. My mother is packing a great picnic for us."

Becky thought quickly. She got off at five. That would give her just enough time to get home, shower and change. "I'll call L.W. right now." She headed for the office. Luckily, the library had slowed down some and Miss Stevenson was presiding over the main desk. The dream dancer had floated away.

"It's Beethoven's Ninth," Edge called after

her. "I know you've heard it a million times—but it should be amusing."

L.W. was free that night and agreed to go with them. Becky went back out to the library and told them everything was set.

"Great!"

"Super!"

Becky suppressed a desire to exclaim, "Terrific!"

"We've got to run," Edge said. "Nice to meet you."

"Nice to meet you."

"I'll pick you up at six," Tom said.

Becky watched them as they exited the library. It had all happened so quickly and unexpectedly. A Beethoven concert! She almost groaned aloud. What did she know about Beethoven? Nothing. She dashed over to the classical music record collection and hunted up a recording of the Ninth. It was three albums long! She would never be able to listen to it on her break.

At three o'clock, Becky went into the small listening room and put the first movement on the stereo. As the music reverberated around the walls of the small room, she read the liner notes. Ludwig Van Beethoven. Born 1770, died 1827. He created nine symphonies, a number of piano concertos, sonatas, string music, music for quartets and many other pieces of music. Then she came to the part about Beethoven going deaf. He was so deaf by the time the Ninth was performed in 1824, that he couldn't even hear the applause of the audience. That was fascinating, she thought, as she listened to the lyrical beginning to the symphony.

The fifteen-minute break was over all too

quickly but Becky decided she would check out the album and listen to it at home while she dressed.

The rest of the afternoon passed quickly. Becky rocketed out of the library at the dot of five. She flew home, and, after checking with her parents and getting their approval for the concert, jumped into the shower.

At five minutes of six, looking elegant and composed, Becky was listening to the second movement of the Ninth and waiting for Tom. Her parents had decided to delay dinner until after her departure.

At six, the front door bell rang. Becky shut off her stereo and went to open the door. Her parents were in the living room, pretending to read the evening paper. Even though they had already met Tom, they were hanging around, waiting to act like parents and do their have-a-good-time, drive-carefully, don't-stay-out-too-late number.

Becky led Tom into the living room. Her mother and father did their number. Tom enacted his I'm-your-daughter's-polite-serious-and-responsible-date-for-the-evening scene and he and Becky made their escape.

As they walked across the grass to the car, Becky wondered if she would do the same routine when she was a parent? Probably, she decided. It seemed to come with the territory.

Tom put his arm lightly around her waist. "You look great," he said.

Becky moved closer to him. "Thank you."

"In fact, you always look great." Tom hugged her close to his side. "I brought Dad's car," he explained as he opened the door to the shiny black BMW. "The Jeep didn't seem right for Beethoven."

"Hi-ho," Edge called cheerfully from the back-seat.

At L.W.'s, Edge went in to pick her up. They emerged in a couple of minutes and got into the car.

"I must say," Edge said, eyeing L.W. approvingly, "Tom said you were good looking, but he didn't say you were this super."

"Thank you," L.W. replied.

Becky was pleased. She hoped they would like each other. "And she's brilliant too," Becky said, turning around in the front seat.

"Not brilliant," L.W. replied modestly, "but I get by."

"Say something in Japanese," Tom coaxed, glancing at her in the rearview mirror.

"Let's see," L.W. said, pondering his request. "I've got it. Sony!"

Tom laughed. "Mitsubishi," he said.

"Toyota," Becky said, joining in the game.

"Honda," Edge cried.

They all laughed. "It's not such a difficult language after all," L.W. said. She turned to Edge. "Are you having a good time in Illinois?"

"Super," he responded. "I'm here for three more days then it's off to California to visit another chum of ours, Duck . . ."

"Duck?" L.W. repeated.

"Duckworth," Tom supplied.

"Is that his first name or his last name?" Becky asked.

"His first name, of course," Edge said. "Then I'm off to Australia."

"Australia?"

"Father has some business to do in Australia," Edge told her, "and I'm going to zip over to meet him. My sister, Duffy, is in China, and she's going to join us. Although one never quite knows if Duff will show up or not." He took his glasses out of his shirt pocket and, holding them by the earpiece, began to twirl them around his fingers.

"Edge is going to do some sailing in Australia," Tom said.

"Stearns here missed the best sailing," Edge said. "It was super in Bar Harbor."

Becky wasn't sure where Bar Harbor was.

As if Tom had read her thoughts, he said, "In Maine. Edge's grandmother has a summer place there."

"Grandmother always summers at the cottage in Bar Harbor," Edge said.

Tom smiled over at Becky. "Translate cottage to mean *very* large house."

"What? What?" Edge asked.

"Cottage means something different out here than it does in Bar Harbor," Tom said. "I was just telling Becky."

"How big is the 'cottage'?" L.W. asked.

Becky was glad L.W. had asked the question. She was dying to know too.

"I don't believe anyone's ever counted the rooms," Edge said. "Twenty-four. Twenty-eight. I really don't know."

Becky was agog at this piece of information. A summer house with twenty-four rooms!

"Edge's grandmother is a formidable lady," Tom said.

"Now, Stearns," Edge admonished him, "she was very nice to you once she found out you were a Remmington."

132

Tom chuckled. "The Remmingtons do come in handy once in awhile."

"The sailing was simply super," Edge repeated.

"Do you travel a lot?" L.W. asked.

"Well," Edge said, putting his glasses back in his pocket, "Mother's off to Florence and Granny's planning her annual pilgrimage to India and . . . yes, I suppose you could say we travel a lot."

L.W. caught Becky's eye. She raised her eyebrows in a do-you-believe-this expression. Becky turned around quickly. She didn't want Edge to see her smile.

Edge turned to L.W. "You must tell me all about school," he said. "How is Mary I. these days?"

"Mary I.?"

"Becky and L.W. go to River Bend High," Tom said quickly.

Becky remembered that Mary Institute was a private girl's school in St. Louis.

"Oh," Edge said, "I just assumed you went there. Well," he said to L.W., "what is River Bend High like?"

L.W. told him briefly about River Bend High.

"We must try it sometime Stearns," Edge said. "It sounds fun."

"I'm going there in the fall," Tom responded. "I told you that."

"Now, Becky," Edge said, leaning forward and resting his elbows on the back of the front seats. "We must talk him out of this. Your school sounds . . . great. But Stearns should come back East to finish school."

"Don't you think that's Tom's decision?" L.W. asked sharply.

Tom pulled the car into the passing lane. "Since I'm living out here now," he said, "I think I ought to stick around and find out more about it."

Edge started to protest.

"We can talk about it later," Tom said.

Edge scooted back into his seat and began to tell L.W. how long his family had been in Boston. "Grandfather started the family bank before the war," he explained.

"Which war?" L.W. asked, puzzled.

"Why, the Revolutionary War," Edge said, as if there had never been any other wars. "The Simpsons have been in Boston for quite a few years. Unlike the Remmingtons," he said, obviously kidding Tom, "who have only been there a short time."

Tom glanced quickly over his shoulder. "Yeah," he said, "we didn't arrive until after the war. I'm afraid we are rather *parvenu* compared to Edge's ancestors."

Edge chuckled.

Becky was surprised to hear Tom talk like that. He had never used a word like *parvenu* around her. She wasn't even quite sure what it meant, though she got the general idea.

Was Edge trying to impress her and L.W. or was he just making casual conversation? She turned to stare out the car window at the passing fields. Edge was like someone from a totally different planet. A world where people had summer "cottages" that were four times as large as the house where Becky lived all the time. A world where people had names like Edge and Duffy and Duck. Where people zipped off to Australia, or China or India.

Edge was telling L.W. something about his

great-great-grandfather. Thinking about Edge's background, and comparing it to her own, Becky was intimidated by the differences between them. Her family had only been in the United States for three generations. Both her great grandfathers had been small-time farmers in Illinois. Before that, she wasn't quite sure where they had been. Somewhere in Germany and England her mother always said. They had been farmers there too.

Becky looked out the window at the landscape. The dilapidated drive-in movie show and the sign for the Happy Homes Trailer Park passed before her as the car zoomed down the highway. What was having three hundred years of family history like? What were servants and summer houses and trips to Florence like? Was it wonderful? Did it make you happy? Edge seemed content. But happier than she and L.W. were?

Becky glanced over at Tom. He was concentrating on the road. Was that the kind of world that Tom had moved through in Boston? His mother's family had been wealthy and prestigious for a long time and yet he seemed different from Edge. He didn't make a big deal out of the Remmingtons or his social history.

"You're very quiet," he said softly, looking over at Becky.

Could she ever enter his world? Becky asked herself. Could she ever learn enough, change enough, to be comfortable in Tom's world? In Edge's world?

Becky looked at Tom's handsome profile and his strong hands as they rested lightly on the steering wheel. Just to be with him was enough. She reached over and put her hand on top of his on the steering wheel.

Tom smiled his incredible smile at her.

"Look," L.W. said, "there's the Arch."

Far across the flat, Illinois fields, the St. Louis Gateway Arch came into view.

Tom navigated the car past downtown St. Louis and in a few minutes they were turning into Forrest Park where the concert was to be held. The park was green and serene as they wound their way through the gently curving roads to the concert site.

It didn't take long to find a parking space. Tom opened the door for Becky and smiled at her as she stepped out of the car. Edge held the door for L.W.

Tom got an enormous picnic hamper out of the trunk and handed a big blanket to Edge. He took Becky's hand and led the way.

As they were about to enter the natural amphitheater, Becky saw Mr. Jones up ahead. The woman he was with looked familiar. The woman turned her head to the side. It was Mrs. Francis! Becky was delighted. They were becoming a twosome. She waved but they didn't see her. She would try and say hello later on, she decided.

The gently sloping hill was already crowded but they managed to find a spot right in the middle.

"We don't want to be too close," Edge said, shaking out the blanket, "or the amplification will be dreadful."

"Of course," L.W. said.

Becky glanced at L.W., trying to read her mood. She had hoped that Edge and L.W. would hit it off. Unfortunately, Edge had talked entirely about himself and his family in the car, and while L.W. had listened politely Becky felt uneasy. It was a blind date and Edge seemed stuffy and overbearing at times. Well, she decided, trying to give Edge a chance, he was probably nervous too. Give him more time, she told herself.

They seated themselves on the blanket and Tom dug into the picnic basket.

"What an absolutely super dinner," Edge said, after they had stuffed themselves on pâté and fresh, crusty French bread; on cold, smoked salmon, a crisp salad and pieces of pale yellow, tangy cheese.

"And for dessert," Tom said, holding up a small confectioner's box with a flourish, "chocolate truffles."

Becky peered inside the box. Nestled inside were eight droplike pieces of chocolate candy.

"Take one covered with white chocolate," Tom said, extending the box to Becky.

Becky had no idea what a truffle was as she lifted one out of the box. Cautiously, she took a bite of the candy. The white chocolate was crunchier than regular chocolate and the inside of the truffle was filled with a thick, rich creamy concoction that had just an edge of tartness to it.

"Aren't they delicious?" Tom asked her.

Becky nodded her head and took another bite. "Amazing." She remembered the Hershey's bars that she had taken on their bike trip. While Becky loved chocolate bars, the truffle was like nothing she had ever tasted before. Was this just another example of the difference between them? She was a Hershey's candy bar girl and Tom was a confectioner's truffles boy? No, she decided, that was totally silly.

"What are you smiling about?" Tom asked.

"Just something dumb," she said. "Please tell your mother how good dinner was."

"I believe the concert is about to begin," Edge announced.

They all looked toward the stage. The musicians were beginning to file out of the wings to take their places.

Becky and L.W. quickly repacked the remains of the picnic into the hamper.

The conductor came out and took his place on the podium. He spoke briefly to the first violinist, raised his arms in the air and the music started. Slow and melodic at first, the sweet sounds of the symphony seemed to wash over them like a gentle, summer breeze.

Tom put his arm around Becky's back and she edged closer to him. This was heaven, she thought. A delicious dinner. Beautiful music. And Tom.

The sun went down and they were enveloped in the warm, velvety luxuriousness of the summer night. Slowly, the music began to build. Becky closed her eyes. This was what she wanted, she thought. To always be with Tom. To feel the fresh crispness of his starched shirt against her cheek, to have his strong arm around her, to be borne away on the strains of the glorious sounding music. Nothing else mattered. Nothing at all.

Tom gently brushed the hair away from the side of Becky's face. She turned her face to his. Tom pressed his lips on hers.

"I say," Edge whispered, "couldn't you two even wait until the second movement?"

Tom chuckled and he and Becky broke their embrace.

"What is the second movement?" he asked.

"If you don't know, Stearns," Edge said, "I certainly can't tell you."

Becky felt as though she should be embarrassed but she wasn't. She leaned back into the warmth of Tom's shoulder.

The music came to a lilting halt. Some of the audience started to applaud. Becky was just about to start clapping when Tom reached over and pinioned her hands.

"You're not supposed to applaud between movements," he whispered in her ear. "Only at the end."

Becky felt a blush creeping up her neck. Why hadn't she known that? she chastised herself. She filed the piece of information away.

The last movement of Beethoven's Ninth Symphony was one of the most incredible pieces of music that Becky had ever heard. She hadn't had time to listen to it at home or during her break. A large choir of men and women filed out onto the stage and took their places behind the musicians. The melodic theme, which had been repeated and had grown in intensity through the first part of the symphony, suddenly, with the addition of the choral voices, sprang to life.

Then it was over, in a rushing, dramatic climax that left Becky gasping, almost breathless.

The audience began applauding. Several people shouted bravo. Becky found herself joining in the applause.

In the car going home, the music was still playing through Becky's head. "That was a wonderful concert," she said, turning to face the backseat. "Thanks for getting the tickets, Edge."

"You're more than welcome," he said. "But

didn't you think the conductor was a bit heavy-handed at times?"

Becky didn't know how to respond. It had all sounded lovely to her.

"What do you think, Stearns?"

"I thought he did a pretty good job," Tom said.

"I prefer Bernstein conducting," Edge said. "He has more vitality; he makes the drama absolutely leap out at you. Don't you agree, L.W.?"

"How right you are," L.W. piped up. "Leonard Bernstein is so much more colorful. His shadings are much more delicate even in the somber moments and," she paused and bit at the skin on her thumb, "there is certainly more power and verve to the bright moments."

"Exactly!" Edge cried.

Where in the world had L.W. heard the Ninth before so that she could talk about it like that? Becky wondered. Edge and L.W. were still discussing the concert. Becky looked out the car window at the dark, flat landscape.

She wished, secretly, that she and Tom had been able to go alone to the concert. She knew that L.W. had not had a good time. In fact, there were a couple of moments when it looked as though L.W. was about to explode. Edge had managed to put his foot in his mouth throughout the evening, but he never seemed to notice that he had said something wrong, or that he had said something that might hurt Becky's or L.W.'s feelings.

How could Tom and Edge be such good friends? They seemed so different. Becky glanced over at Tom. He raised his eyebrow as if to ask if anything was the matter. Becky shook her head and smiled at him. He turned back to the highway.

Becky decided that she would not worry about Edge. She would think about the concert and Tom's kiss. She settled back more comfortably in her seat and watched the dark, verdant fields as the car sped home toward River Bend.

# 10

**W**hat a pompous, self-centered geek," L.W. raged into the telephone. "I've never met anyone who was so concerned with himself and where he's been and where he's going and . . ."

Becky had been on the phone for ten minutes with L.W. and she had never heard her so angry about anyone before.

"Simpson Malcolm Edgington can go right back where he came from," L.W. said emphatically, "I don't care if I never see him again as long as I live."

"It's Malcolm Edgington Simpson," Becky corrected her.

"I don't care!"

"I'm sorry you had a bad time."

"I didn't have a terrible time," L.W. said, calming down somewhat. "The music was lovely, the picnic was delicious, Tom's a nice guy . . . but he sure has a disgusting best friend . . ."

Becky wanted to head the conversation away from Edge. "The music was beautiful, wasn't it?"

"I'm surprised you remember the music at all," L.W. said, "you and Tom were so wrapped up in each other."

Becky smiled. "I didn't know you knew so much about music," she said, changing the subject. "Where did you learn about verve and brightness and all that?"

"I don't know anything about music," L.W. said, laughing, "even if I did take piano lessons for six years. All you have to do is throw around enough adjectives and everybody thinks you're an expert."

"You sure sounded like one."

"I just couldn't stand another minute of Mr. Malcolm's tripe."

"He was impressed."

"He should have been a lot more impressed," L.W. stated, the anger coming back into her voice. "Here we are, two of the most beautiful girls in River Bend, and he tries to bore us to death."

Was that the problem? Becky asked herself. Because they were just two girls from River Bend? Would Edge have acted differently if she and L.W. had been two girls who went to private school in St. Louis?

"Do you think he's like that all the time?" L.W. asked. "Or was he just trying to impress us?"

"I think he's like that all the time," Becky answered. "It's just the way he is."

"It's not a great way to be," L.W. said. She sounded less angry. "You're right," Becky said. She looked out the window of her bedroom. It was a rare, rainy summer Sunday. She wondered how Tom and Edge would spend it.

"What are you going to do today?" L.W. asked.

"I'm sort of hoping Tom will call."

"And spend another day with Edge?"

Becky felt that she should try to be loyal to Tom's best friend. "He's just different from us."

"He sure is different," L.W. said. "He's a jerk." L.W. paused for several seconds. When she spoke again, her voice was serious. "Be careful, Becky."

"What do you mean?" Becky asked.

"As nice as Tom is," L.W. said cautiously, "he seemed different around Edge last night."

Becky started to protest.

"I know Tom is a nice guy," L.W. said, hurrying on, "but you've made a lot of changes in yourself since you met him—not bad changes—and he seems to really like you but I don't think Edge is a good influence."

"What do you mean?"

"People like Edge," L.W. began, "with all that money and family and things, are sort of careless, I think. Edge is insulated from the real world. If he cared a little more, he would have made an effort to get to know you and me better last night. But he's Malcolm Edgington Simpson the Third from Boston and he doesn't have to make an effort. He'll breeze off to California and Australia and won't give us another thought."

"But Tom's not like that."

"I know, I know," L.W. said. "But be careful of Edge. I don't trust him."

"All right." Becky said. Though she didn't completely agree with L.W., she respected her opinion.

"I've got to go," L.W. said. "We're going to my grandmother's for supper."

"L.W.?"

"Yes?"

"Thanks for going last night. I'm sorry you didn't have a better time."

"I had an all right time. It was just the awful Edge that was the problem."

Becky smiled at her friend's description. "Bye," she said, hanging up the phone. She got up and put the recording of the Ninth on her stereo. The incredible music—last night's music—rolled out of the speakers.

Becky wanted Edge to go away and for her and Tom to be together again. She wanted her Tom back. The handsome guy with the bicycle and the Irish Setter. The guy who could flip a Frisbee like an expert, who knew about science and books, who she could talk to about the novels she read.

But was that possible? Was it all just a summer dream? When school started, would Tom fit in with the other kids? He certainly had at the pool that day but would he be out of place at River Bend High? Would the differences between Tom and Becky eventually reach a point where Becky would be an embarrassment to him?

Becky slowly ran her finger along the top of the telephone. She wouldn't let that happen. She would continue to grow and change. She would dazzle Tom with her intelligence and her accumulating knowledge. Maybe, just maybe, what he liked about her was that fact that she was different from all the girls he had known before.

The phone rang, interrupting her thoughts. Becky picked up the receiver.

"Edge and I are just sitting around this afternoon," Tom said. "Why don't you come over and we'll play scrabble or something?" He paused.

Becky could just picture him running his hand through the side of his hair.

"I hope you don't have plans," he added.

"That sounds like fun," Becky said.

"Do you think L.W. would like to join us?"

"She has to go to her grandmother's," Becky said quickly.

"That's too bad. Edge liked her."

That was ironic, Becky thought. No way, could L.W. be persuaded to spend an afternoon with Edge.

"I'll pick you up in . . . twenty minutes. O.K.?"

"Fine. See you."

She went to tell her mother where she was going. Todd was in the family room, watching a baseball game on the television. He glanced up from the screen and did a double take.

"Marion," he said, "you look like a Girl Scout."

"Poor Todd," Becky said, "if only you knew how chic and sophisticated your sister has become."

"Yeah," he demanded, "tell me about it?" He held his fingers up to his eyes and pretended to be squinting through a pair of thick lenses. "All you need is a pair of glasses and a butterfly net."

"I refuse to sink to your level of juvenile

banter," Becky said haughtily. She walked over and peered out the window in the family room door.

Somebody on television hit a double and Todd turned his attention back to the game. Tom pulled into the driveway.

"Bye everybody," Becky called. She darted out the door to meet him.

Tom had the top on the Jeep. The sound of the rain on the roof of the car reminded Becky of the patter of the rain on Tom's poncho. She wished that they could just drive out into the wet countryside and be alone together.

"I had a great time last night," Tom said. "Isn't Edge great?"

"Uh-huh," Becky answered. "I had a nice time too."

Tom was in high spirits. He rattled on about how much fun he and Edge were having and how much he had missed him.

Doesn't he see Edge for what he is? Becky asked herself. Selfish and pretentious. Becky knew that Tom and Edge had been friends since they were kids. Was Tom so close to him that he was blind to Edge's faults? Maybe, Becky thought, Edge was different when he and Tom were together.

Tom parked the Jeep in the driveway of his house and they dodged the rain and ran up onto the side porch. Mr. and Mrs. Stearns were in the kitchen.

"Hello Becky," Mr. Stearns said, standing up and smiling at her. "Nice to see you again."

Mrs. Stearns only smiled coolly.

"Hello," Becky said.

Tom led the way out of the kitchen to the front

porch. Edge was lounging in a wicker chair reading a section of the Sunday newspaper. "Hi-ho, Becky," he said. He tossed the paper disdainfully to the floor. "Grandfather knew the founder of the paper," he said, referring to the St. Louis newspaper, "and I must say that it hasn't improved with age." He looked at Becky. "How do you survive without *The New York Times?*"

Becky was determined to be polite. "I see it at the library, you know." The library did get the *Times* but Becky never read it. She mentally crossed her fingers and hoped Edge didn't pursue the topic.

"That's one solution," he responded. "I suppose."

"Let's play scrabble," Tom said, sounding hearty and like a sports announcer.

They sat down at one of Mrs. Stearn's white wicker tables and started to play. Tom and Edge were both good players and were highly competitive. Tom won the first game and Becky won the next two.

Becky was really proud of herself when she was able to make the word "vague" and get a double score in the bargain.

"I concede to the new champion," Tom said. "You creamed us, Becky."

Becky started to say, "I was just lucky," but changed her mind and said, "Shall I give you two another chance to redeem yourselves?"

"No," Edge said, "I've had enough scrabble." He stood up from the table and walked over to the side of the porch. It was still drizzling. "What a dreary day."

Becky excused herself to go to the bathroom. On her way back to the front porch, she paused in the hall and looked into the living room. It was a lovely room. The richly colored oriental carpet, the chairs and tables and the lamps and vases all blended into a formal, yet inviting looking room. And the whole pattern was presided over by the Sargent portrait of Mrs. Remmington. It was the kind of room where elegantly dressed people would sip tea and talk about literature and philosophy, Becky decided.

With a sigh, Becky turned from the room. She was just about to open the front screen door, when she heard Edge say:

"Becky's hardly the person for you to be dating."

Becky stood frozen to the spot.

"You sound like my mother," Tom said. "Becky's a really nice girl."

"Your mother is a very smart woman," Edge said. He paused. "I didn't say Becky wasn't nice, but admit it, Tom, you were in a new town, lonely and she's just a little librarian that you happened to meet."

Tom said something that Becky couldn't hear.

"Imagine her in Boston?" Edge said. "Imagine introducing her to the other guys at school."

"She'd be fine."

"Are you sure?"

"Of course."

At least, Becky thought, Tom was sticking up for her.

"I know you can't do anything about your parents moving out to this, this cornfield," Edge said, "but why get involved with the farmer's daughter?"

"You've got to stop talking about Becky like that," Tom said, angrily.

"I'm your best friend. I'm only saying it because I think you need to hear it."

"Did Mom put you up to this?"

"She mentioned it," Edge admitted.

Becky fled back to the bathroom. She forced herself not to cry. How dare Edge—crummy, stuck-up Edge—talk about her like that? How dare he try and take Tom away from her? And Tom's mother felt the same way. That's why she had been so cool when Becky came into the house.

Suddenly all Becky could think of was getting back to the sanctuary of her parent's cozy little house and the security of her own safe room.

She rinsed her face with cold water and ran her hands through her hair. She would tell Tom she had a headache. It wasn't a great excuse but it would have to do. She would say goodbye to Edge, hope she never saw him again in her entire life and have Tom take her home. Quickly.

Somehow, she got through her goodbye with Edge and got herself into the Jeep with Tom. She was silent on the way back to her house.

"Are you all right?"

"I just don't feel too good."

"You're sure a whiz at scrabble," Tom said.

Tell me it's not true, Becky begged Tom silently. Take me in your arms and hold me and wipe out all the rotten things that Edge just said.

"Edge is going to be here until Wednesday," Tom said. "We're going to be pretty busy." He pulled the car into Becky's driveway. "But maybe we could get together on Wednesday night."

He didn't suspect that she had overheard their conversation, Becky realized. She couldn't bring herself to tell him either. Becky didn't want to talk about the things Edge had said. She knew that they weren't true but what if Tom secretly thought they were true? At least, she consoled herself, he wanted to see her again.

"Sure," Becky said, opening the door and getting out of the car.

"I hope you feel better. I'll call you."

Becky let herself into the house. It was quiet. Her parents were out to dinner with friends and Todd was spending the night at Jake's. She was glad she was alone. Becky wanted to cry; wanted to scream and beat her fists against the wall. No, what she really wanted to do was punch Malcolm Edgington Simpson as hard as she could.

Should she call L.W.? No, L.W. wasn't home. She couldn't call Laurie K. Laurie K. might do something rash like go directly to Tom's and tell Edge exactly what she thought of him.

Becky took two aspirin tablets and wandered through the empty rooms of the house. She found herself in the Johnsons' living room. Becky's mother had splurged two years ago and completely redecorated the room. At the time, Becky had loved the new blue wall-to-wall carpeting, the soft Italian Provincial couches and chairs and the sleek new fruitwood tables. She especially loved the reproductions of the Andrew Wyeth paintings that her mother had framed and hung on the walls.

But now, looking at it and comparing it to the Stearns' living room, Becky wasn't sure if it was a nice room or not. Did it look new and modern and—she hated to even think the word—cheap? Were the furnishings and the pictures common and ordinary?

No, she thought, feeling disloyal to her parents,

151

her mother had spent a lot of time and money to get everything exactly right. It was a pretty room. *It was*.

Becky sat down on the couch. She was tired. So tired she didn't want to think about anything anymore. She didn't want to think about Edge or the Stearns or the Remmingtons or John Singer Sargent or Beethoven or . . .

The ringing telephone woke Becky. It was dark outside. For a second, she didn't know where she was. Then she realized she had fallen asleep on the couch. She groped her way to the kitchen and answered the phone.

"Hi," Tom said. "How are you feeling?"

"Better."

"I was worried about you."

"Too much scrabble, I guess." Becky tried to sound lighthearted.

"I'm glad you're feeling better."

"Let's make plans to do something Wednesday night," Tom suggested.

Becky's heart gave a feeble little leap. He did like her. It didn't matter what Edge had said.

"Let's do something you want to do," Tom said. "I've had enough concerts and culture."

Becky thought quickly. It would be wonderful to do something different from the things they had been doing. Something that would completely obliterate Edge's presence from River Bend. What could she suggest? A movie. A baseball game. Were the Cardinals in town? Then it came to her. But would Tom like the idea?

"Let's go cruising, the great American pastime."

"Great," Tom said, sounding enthusiastic. "What time should we start?"

"Why don't you pick me up at nine," Becky said.

"Great. Are you sure you're O.K?"

"Yes," Becky said. "Really. I'm fine."

"See you Wednesday."

Becky hung up the phone and wandered back to her room. The pain of Edge's comments still hurt but Tom's calling and making their upcoming date helped to ease that pain. She had to go on seeing Tom. She liked him too much—no matter what Edge or his parents thought.

Becky sat down on her bed and drew her legs up under her. She hugged her pillow to her stomach. She picked up a copy of another Edith Wharton novel that she had checked out of the library. She opened the book but her mind wasn't on reading. She and Tom were just a guy and a girl who liked each other. They weren't characters in some novel. Why couldn't everybody just leave them alone?

She balanced the book on her knees. Well, Edge would be gone in three days and then maybe everything would go back to the way it was supposed to be. She turned her attention to the novel.

Over the next few days, Becky tried to put Edge's comments out of her mind. But she found herself coming back to them at odd moments. When the scene on the porch cropped up in her thoughts, she would tromp it down hard in her mind and try not to think about it. Instead, she would think about her coming date with Tom. She didn't mention the scene to anyone because she thought her parents would probably be hurt and angry and might forbid her to see Tom again. She kept it all to herself and tried to forget.

Before she knew it, it was Wednesday night and she and Tom were in the Jeep. Tom leaned over to kiss her briefly. "I've missed you," he said.

"I've missed you too," Becky responded.

As they backed out of the driveway, Tom turned on the tape player.

Becky turned up the volume. "The music has to be loud," she said. "And it should be coming from the back speakers."

Tom turned a knob and a sexy male voice boomed from the speakers hidden in the back. "Like that?"

"You're learning."

"Where do we go?"

"First," Becky said, considering the question, "we ought to drive by the Dairy Bar. It's a little early and we should just take a quick look to see if anybody's there."

There was only one car in the lot of the Dairy Bar and Becky didn't recognize it.

"Let's do the circuit on this side of town," Becky suggested. "First, Fish 'n Chips."

The Fish 'n Chips lot was also deserted but just as they were about to pull out into the traffic, a red convertible flashed by.

"Quick," Becky squealed, "honk."

Tom pressed the horn down.

L.W. saw them, did a screeching U-turn, and pulled into the lot.

"She's got Christopher Ralston with her," Becky said, recognizing the guy in the front seat.

L.W. parked next to Tom's Jeep.

"Look who I found limping along the highway," L.W. said, indicating the guy sitting next to her.

"I think I twisted something," Christopher said, smiling at Becky and Tom. He was a cute junior guy who was a dedicated runner and the star of the track team at school.

Becky introduced Tom and Christopher.

"How's Edge?" L.W. asked.

Becky hoped she wasn't going to say something awful.

"He left this afternoon," Tom replied.

"Good," L.W. said. "I mean, I'm glad he got off safely," she said quickly. "What are you two doing tonight?"

"Becky's introducing me to the pleasures of cruising."

"It's about time," L.W. said. "I've got to get our track star here home and into a hot compress." She turned to Christopher. "Or is it a cold compress?"

"Hot," he replied.

L.W. started her car. "Maybe we'll see you later." She roared out of the parking lot.

"Now that's interesting," Becky said.

"What?"

"Christopher. With L.W. He's kind of shy and is super dedicated to track—he won several important meets last year. They might make a good pair."

"Are you going to play matchmaker?"

"It never hurts," Becky said.

Tom smiled at her. "What's next?"

"Since we're on this side of town, we ought to check out the other places over here."

"You're the boss," Tom said, starting the engine.

Becky directed Tom through the parking lot of the Pizza Hut. It too was almost deserted. "It's too early," she informed him. "People don't eat pizza until before they go home."

Next was Burger King. It was filled with a Little League baseball team and a few tired-looking adults. The A & W was empty. The car hops were chatting and leaning on the counters inside.

"We could drive out to the video arcade and the movie house parking lot," Becky said, trying to decide on their next move. "There might be a lot more people out now."

Tom turned the Jeep toward the small shopping mall. Becky put another tape into the player.

There were a couple of cars that Becky recognized in the arcade parking lot but nobody worth stopping for. The parking lot of the cinema was almost deserted too. Not many people went to the movies on Wednesday night.

"Not very exciting out here," Tom said.

Becky agreed. "But you have to check it out," she said. "Just in case."

"In case of what?"

Becky was stumped for a moment. "Well," she said, "in case somebody's got a secret date with somebody they shouldn't have, and we might spot them. Or we might run into somebody that we haven't seen in a long time, or . . ." it was hard to explain the reasons. "But the main reason," Becky said, "is to kill time. To enjoy the evening and just enjoy driving around."

"But couldn't you just kill time at home?"

"It's not the same. Let's go back to the other

side of town. Things should be more lively over there."

Just as they were pulling out of the parking lot, Jeff's Trans-Am zipped past them.

"Quick," Becky shouted, "follow that car."

"Which one?"

"The Trans-Am. It's Jeff and Laurie K."

Tom screeched out of the lot. A little old lady in a Toyota honked her horn and yelled something at them as Tom pulled in front of her.

Tom grinned at Becky; Becky grinned back.

The Trans-Am was three cars ahead of them. "They're turning into MacDonald's," Becky said. "Follow them."

Tom pulled into the lot. There were six or seven cars already there, with kids either sitting on the hoods of their cars or lounging in the front seats.

Tom pulled next to Jeff and Laurie K. and stopped.

"Hi, Jeff," Becky called.

"How you doin', Becky?"

Laurie K. leaned across Jeff and said hello.

"Hi," Tom called.

"What's happenin'?" Jeff asked.

"Not much," Becky replied.

"Yeah," Jeff agreed, "we're just roamin' around."

Conversation with Jeff did not exactly tax one's mental capacity.

They all got out and leaned on the front of Jeff's car.

"The Cardinals are really cookin'," Jeff said to Tom. "Did you see the game against the Mets?"

Becky tensed up. Was Jeff baiting Tom? She waited for Tom's reply.

"It was incredible, wasn't it?" Tom said. "The triple in the fifth inning put them over the top."

"It was far out," Jeff agreed.

Jeff and Tom discussed the intricacies of the recent baseball game.

Becky told Laurie K. about seeing L.W. and Christopher Ralston together. One of the necessities of cruising was keeping everybody up to date on everybody else's movements.

"You're kidding?" Laurie K. exclaimed. "That may be the opportunity she's been waiting for."

Then Becky saw Jonathan pull into the lot. What was he doing home? He parked on the other side of Jeff's car and got out and walked over.

"Yo, Jonathan," Jeff called.

"I didn't know you were in town," Laurie K. said.

"I just got in this evening," he answered. "The last session starts on Sunday and I had a few days off, so I decided to come home. Hi, Becky," he said.

Becky felt a rush of anxiety down in her stomach. How would Tom and Jonathan get along? Laurie K. introduced them. Becky could tell that Jonathan was carefully checking Tom out but since Tom didn't know about him, he was just another guy to him.

"What a cool Jeep," Jonathan said. "Is it yours?"

"Sort of," Tom replied.

"How do you like River Bend?"

Becky knew that Laurie K. had kept Jonathan up-to-date on her activities with Tom.

"I like it," Tom said.

"You're from Boston?"

Becky looked at Tom and Jonathan together. Tom was tall, but Jonathan was taller. Tom was more muscular looking than Jonathan, but Jonathan looked lean and healthy as he propped himself against the fender of Jeff's car.

"How did you get Tom out cruising?" Laurie K. whispered.

Becky glanced away from the guys. "I just suggested it."

"It's about time," Laurie K. said. "After all those plays and concerts that you've been going to."

Becky glanced back over at Tom. The guys were discussing the recent baseball game again. Tom's strong profile was silhouetted against the lights. None of it mattered at all, she decided, there in the parking lot of MacDonald's. Becky felt that special pride of possession that people feel when they're with someone whom they like and of whom they are proud.

Mary and Debbie and Monica showed up in Mary's cool new Firebird. Becky reintroduced Tom to them. He remembered them from the pool and was at ease and seemed to be enjoying himself. Then Debbie started flirting with Tom and Becky decided that it was time to go.

"I know where there's a party," Jeff said. "Why don't you come with us?"

"Thanks," Becky said, "but we're going to drive around some more."

They pulled out of the lot and headed back to the other side of town. As they drove through the parking lots of the places on the first circuit, Tom seemed distracted, as if he was thinking about something.

"Is something on your mind?" Becky asked.

She had almost been afraid to ask the question, afraid of what his answer might be.

"No, no," Tom said hastily. "I was just thinking about . . . it's not important."

"Do you want to talk about it?"

He shook his head and turned the Jeep back onto the main road. "I never realized there were so many places to check out," Tom said, turning to smile at Becky.

"Are you having a good time?"

"Sure," Tom said. "It's not quite what I was expecting but . . ."

"What did you think it would be like?"

"You know," Tom said, "more drama—more action. Cruising is really just everybody out, hanging out. Isn't it?"

"That's the whole point," Becky said.

Was Tom having a boring time? Of course, he didn't know most of the kids and didn't know their cars so it wasn't as much fun for him as it was for Becky and the regulars.

Becky began to feel that maybe the evening had been a failure. She wanted to try and salvage it somehow. "Oh, there's drama," she said. "If a guy and a girl have a fight then everybody sort of gets involved. You have to listen to both sides of the argument and try and help them track each other down. Jeff and Laurie K. do that a lot," Becky admitted. "Or, once in a while, a car of guys from a rival high school shows up and there might be a fight or something—but not very often," she added. Becky felt like she was sinking deeper and deeper into a mire. "Then, sometimes, one of the guys might drink too much and you have to help sober him up and get him home in one piece and . . . there's a lot of excitement," she concluded lamely.

Tom listened carefully to her explanation but he didn't make a comment.

Becky thought that most of the kids were probably going to the party that Jeff had mentioned. Should she suggest that they go too? The parties were generally pretty much fun but perhaps Tom wouldn't enjoy it.

"Hey," Tom said, trying to bring some excitement into his voice, "we left out Dog 'n Suds." He turned the Jeep toward the restaurant. They swung through the parking lot.

"Are you hungry?"

"Not really," Becky answered. "Are you?"

Tom shrugged.

"We could go back to the MacDonald's lot," Becky said hopefully. "There's probably a whole new bunch of kids there now."

"Do you want to?"

"If you do."

"Maybe we should call it a night," Tom said.

Becky glanced at the clock on the dashboard. It was only 11:00 P.M.

"I'm kind of tired," Tom said. "It was a busy week, with Edge and all."

"It's kind of an off night," Becky said, trying to sound not too disappointed. "It's better on the weekends."

She couldn't figure out the change in Tom. He had been having a good time at the beginning of the evening and he had seemed to enjoy their stop at MacDonald's and the other kids.

He turned the Jeep into the subdivision where Becky lived and headed toward her house.

Had he been dreadfully bored? She wished that he would say something, give her some clue to why he was so quiet.

He pulled the Jeep into her driveway and shut off the engine and the lights. The house was dark.

"I had a good time," he said, turning to her.

"You did great," Becky said, trying to sound lighthearted. "It'll be more fun when you know all the kids."

Tom leaned over and kissed her. He held her tight for several moments, stroking her hair with his hand. Then he pulled away and climbed out of the car.

At the door, he said, "I'll call you."

"I'm sorry the evening wasn't more exciting."

"It was fun." But his words sounded more polite than enthusiastic. "Good night."

Becky let herself into the house. After a whole exciting week with Edge, was cruising the last thing on earth that Becky should have suggested they do? Becky wished that there had been more kids out, wished that something novel and interesting had happened.

She sighed as she changed into her nightgown. One evening wasn't going to ruin their relationship. Although she did wish that she knew more about what had been on Tom's mind. It was the first time since she had known him that he had seemed distant.

## 11

One night, near the middle of August, Tom called Becky about nine o'clock.

"I've got to talk to you," he said. "Can I come over?"

Becky's stomach gave a lurch. "What's the matter?"

"I don't want to talk about it on the phone. Can I come over?"

"Of course," Becky said. "But my parents have company and Jake is here . . . could you pick me up?"

"I'll be there in five minutes. All right?"

"Yes."

Becky hung up the receiver. Suddenly, she was petrified. His voice had a strained quality to it. What could be the matter? Was something wrong between them? Had she been too blinded by her feelings for him to catch the signals that he had been sending? She hadn't seen him for a couple of days because he was finishing up his science course at Abercrombie and he said he had some things to do with his parents.

Becky searched her mind back through the past week, looking for anything—a gesture, a glance, a hesitation—that would give her a clue to the reason for this meeting. She could not come up with a single reason.

They had had such a good time together after Edge had gone to California. Even though the evening of cruising hadn't been one hundred percent successful, Becky and Tom had taken a long bike ride out into the countryside and pic-nicked under a tree, had taken Maxwell back to the park for some exercise and had gone to the movies just three days ago. Everything had been fine. Tom had seemed like his usual, spirited self.

Nervously, Becky checked her makeup. She picked up her purse and went to tell her parents that she was going out for awhile.

She told her mother that Tom was picking her up, said goodnight to her parent's guests, and went outside to wait for Tom.

A car pulled up in front of the house and stopped. Becky didn't know who it was. Where was Tom and the Jeep? Then she realized that it was Tom and that he was driving his father's BMW. Becky took a deep breath and walked across the yard.

Tom was getting out on the driver's side.

"Hi," she said, trying to sound nonchalant.

Tom looked grim. "I'm sorry to call you on such short notice."

"That's O.K. I wasn't doing anything."

They both got in and Tom started the car.

Becky was miserable. Should she wait for him to bring it up or should she just ask him outright? She didn't think she could stand the tension much longer.

Tom stopped the car at a yield sign. He turned to look at her. "Could we get a soda or something? I don't want to talk and drive around."

Becky nodded.

"A & W?"

Becky nodded again. Then Tom leaned over and kissed her. It was just a quick peck on the lips. Instead of reassuring Becky, it made her more nervous.

They were silent until they had turned into the A & W and pulled into a parking space. At least it wasn't crowded, Becky thought.

"Do you want a root beer?" Tom asked.

Becky didn't want a root beer. She wanted Tom. And she had a terrible feeling that she was about to lose him.

"No . . . yes."

Tom leaned out to the speaker and ordered two large root beers.

They sat in silence. In a couple of minutes the carhop was on the way with their order.

Becky knew the girl from high school. The girl smiled at Tom as she set the tray down. He smiled at her, gave her some money and told her to keep the change.

"Thanks," she said. She leaned down and peered in the window. "Hi, Becky."

"Hi."

"How are you?"

"Fine . . . how are you?"

"I'm fine. Looking forward to the start of school?"

Becky was going to scream in about two seconds if the girl didn't leave and let her find out what Tom had to say.

"Yes. It's nice to see you."

Tom was watching Becky. Just before she straightened up, the girl winked at Becky, as if to say, "What a fox!"

Tom handed Becky her drink. He left his own on the tray outside. He turned to face her.

"I don't know how to say this."

"Please. Just say it."

He took a deep breath. "I have to go back to school."

Becky's first thought was one of pure joy. He's not breaking up with me.

"I have to leave next week. Wednesday."

Then Becky realized what he was saying. He was going away. "But I thought you were going to River Bend High?"

"I wanted to. I want to. But my parents insist that I go back East."

"Why?"

"They think it's a better school . . . and that it would be hard to start a new school in my senior year . . . and that River Bend would hurt me academically and . . ."

"It's not such a bad school," Becky said, feeling loyal to River Bend. "Refuse to go." She had meant for her voice to sound strong but it came out sounding like a wail.

"I have. I've been arguing with my parents ever since Edge left. It's been terrible."

166

Edge! The awful Edge. Was he behind this? "Why didn't you tell me?"

"I couldn't. If I ended up staying here, I didn't want to worry you. And if I did go back . . . well, I didn't want to spoil our last few days together."

"You should have told me." That was it, she realized. It was the conflict of whether he stayed in River Bend or whether he went back to prep school that had been on his mind. "Why did you want to go to River Bend in the first place?" Becky had never asked that question before.

"I thought it would be good for me," he said slowly. "I thought it would give me a chance to see a different side of life. To get away from, from my family—in a way."

Was he rebelling against the Remmingtons? Becky remembered his conversation in his bedroom the day they painted. Could Tom be trying to break away from his family of "over-achievers"?

"But we can still see each other," she said. "You'll be home for Thanksgiving, Christmas. And maybe I could come and visit and I'm a great letter writer and . . ."

"That's just it," he said. "You're going to be a junior. You've got two more years of high school. You shouldn't be tied down to a guy that's a thousand miles away."

"That doesn't matter to me."

Tom put his head back on the steering wheel.

"It'll go really quickly," Becky said. "You'll be home next summer. The school year will be over before we know it."

Tom sat up and looked at her. "That's the point," he said. "Long-distance relationships don't work." He took a deep breath. "I don't think we should go on seeing each other. Not the way we have been."

There it was. Finally. His words hung in the air between them like the spectre of a horrible nightmare.

"Do you want to break up with me?"

"We have to. These things never work long-distance. I know. I've tried it. I met a girl last year who went to school in Manhattan. We went together for a couple of months and it was crazy. Crazy. I hated being so far away from her and I hated being alone and I hated going to visit and . . ."

"But we're different."

"It'd end up being the same crummy situation, Becky. You would want to go to dances and the football games and the prom, and I'd want to go out and we'd feel guilty if we went . . . and lonely if we didn't go."

"I wouldn't."

"Believe me," Tom said. "You would."

"How do you know how I'd feel?"

"I'm sorry. I know how I felt."

"How come you never told me about this girl in Manhattan?"

"It didn't seem important."

Becky had a horrible thought. "Do you want to see her again?"

"No," Tom said, shaking his head.

"Is there someone else?"

"No," Tom said. "There's no one else."

Becky looked at Tom's profile as he stared out the windshield. She wanted to memorize his strong, straight nose, the hair around his temples, his long eyelashes and the way his eyebrows arched gracefully in the middle. She looked at his strong hands as they gripped the steering wheel, his wrists which extended beyond his turned-up shirt sleeves.

Could she give him up? How could she give up all the wonderful summer afternoons that they had spent together?

She started to say the three words that she had wanted to say for the past two months, that she had been afraid to articulate. "I . . . I . . ."

Tom stiffened in the seat. His knuckles turned white. "I like you a lot, Becky," he said, staring straight ahead. "More than I've ever liked anyone . . . but it just won't work."

"Couldn't we try?"

"No."

His voice was so final sounding, so definite, that Becky did what she had sworn to herself, all evening, she would not do. She began to cry. She pulled her purse onto her lap and began to dig through it.

"There's some Kleenex in the glove compartment."

"Please," Becky pleaded, "let's go." She handed her untouched root beer back to him.

Tom started the car and backed out of the parking space. When they reached the street, where it was dark, Becky opened the glove compartment and pulled out several tissues. She tried to will herself to stop crying.

As they drove under a street lamp, she looked over at Tom. He was looking straight ahead. His face was pale and strained looking.

Becky dabbed at her eyes and blew her nose. She was glad that it was dark and that they were in his father's car. She could not have endured having the conversation in the Jeep. That wonderful, copper-colored Jeep that had whisked her into a new world of summer. Becky scooted over in her seat so that she was as close to the door as she could get. The ride home seemed to take forever.

When they pulled up in front of her parent's house, the image of the Stearns family came washing over Becky. She was visited by yet another horrible thought. His parents were behind this. It wasn't just Tom going back to school. It was to get him away from River Bend and away from Becky. And Edge was responsible too.

Tom turned off the engine. He didn't move.

Becky looked over at him, then over at her parent's house. It was a nice house, she thought. There was a light on in her parent's bedroom and a light in the den. She loved them.

"Is it because of me?" she asked.

"What do you mean?" Tom looked at her for the first time since they had left A & W.

"Because of who I am? Because we aren't on the same level—socially."

"What makes you think that?" Tom demanded.

"We're different," Becky said. It hurt to actually say those words, to admit them. "I don't know very much about most of the things that you and your parents are interested in and we don't have as much money and . . ."

"You think I spend all my time at school hanging out with royalty?" Tom said.

"No," Becky said, a flash of anger burning clear and sharp in her mind. "Just people like Edge."

"I'm sorry," Tom said.

She had finally mentioned his name. She couldn't stop herself. "Did Edge have something to do with this?"

"What do you mean?"

"About you going back to school? About breaking up with me?"

"He's glad I'm coming back."

All the anger that Becky had repressed, and all the hurt, after she had overheard their conversation, came washing back over her. "I bet he's glad that you're breaking up with 'the farmer's daughter',," she said bitterly.

The color drained from Tom's face. "You heard him say that?"

"Yes."

"I'm sorry, Becky," Tom said. "Edge didn't mean it, he . . ."

"He did mean it," she said, "every word of it. And about your mother too."

"No, he . . . I . . . . Please . . . could we stop talking about it?"

"That's fine with me." Becky said.

"Can I call you tomorrow?"

"No," Becky said. "Don't."

Becky climbed out of the car and stumbled across the yard to the front stoop. As she was trying to put her key in the lock, she heard Tom start the car. Please, she prayed, let him leap out of the car and come up and tell me it's all a bad dream. That none of it is true. She heard the car drive away.

Once inside, she closed the front door and hurried down the hall to her room. "I'm home," she said to her parent's closed bedroom door. She hoped her voice didn't sound as strange to them as it sounded to her. "I'm exhausted. See you in the morning."

She hurried into her bedroom and closed the door. Becky went numb. She didn't think she even had the energy to turn on the light. She stood there in the darkness for several minutes, looking straight ahead, her mind blank. Finally, she forced herself to switch on the light.

She hung up her skirt and blouse in the closet and slipped into her robe. Sitting down on her bed, she picked up her novel, but the pages were all a blur to her.

She thought of bringing the phone into her room and calling Laurie K. It would be nice to have someone sympathetic to talk it all out with. She glanced at the clock. It was 10:00 P.M. Could her whole life have changed so much in one hour?

She tiptoed into the hall and dragged the phone into her room. Laurie K. answered on the third ring.

"Could you come over?" Becky asked.

"What's the matter?"

Becky didn't think she could speak. She closed her eyes and forced out the words, "Tom and I broke up."

"Jeff's here," Laurie K. said. "Let me kick him out and I'll be right over."

"I don't want to interrupt."

"Are you crazy? I'll be right there."

Becky set the phone down by her bed and picked up her novel again. She tried to concentrate but couldn't.

There was a tap on her door. Her mother stuck her head in. "I just thought I'd say good night. Did you and Tom have a good time?"

"It was all right." Becky looked at the book

quickly, hoping her mother wouldn't notice that she had been crying.

"What's the matter?"

"Nothing."

Her mother came into the room and gently shut the door. "Did you and Tom have a fight?"

"No," Becky said, her voice breaking, "we didn't have a fight. We . . . we broke up."

Her mother sat down on the side of the bed and stroked Becky's knee through the material of her robe. "Do you want to talk about it?"

"No."

"Sure?"

"Oh," Becky wailed, "he has to go back to school in the East, and he doesn't want to see me anymore. At least, not as a girlfriend." Becky told her a little about their awful discussion in the car.

"How do you feel about it?" her mother asked.

"I don't want to break up."

"Boston is a long way away," Mrs. Johnson said, "and . . ."

If she says, "It's probably for the best," Becky knew that she was going to scream. "Laurie K.'s coming over," Becky said quickly.

Her mother leaned over and kissed her on the forehead. "Just remember that we love you," she said. "And if you need us, we're here." She let herself out of the room silently.

Laurie K. came striding in a few minutes later. "Tom's a jerk," she said decisively, "a giant jerk."

Becky put down her book and Laurie K. came over and hugged her.

"I'm really sorry," she said. "What happened?"

Becky started with the telephone call and told Laurie K. the whole story. She felt a little better, being able to talk about it.

"It's too bad," Laurie K. said. "I know how much you liked him and he seemed to really like you."

"What I can't understand," Becky said, "is why we can't go on seeing each other. Even if he is going to be away."

"But remember Mary?" Laurie K. asked.

Mary Black was a junior who had been a part of their group for a while last winter.

"Remember how it was when Greg went off to the University of Colorado? And Mary was lonely and sort of depressed and hung around with us all the time? Then Greg didn't come home for Thanksgiving because he went skiing . . . and was only home for a week at Christmas."

Becky remembered how miserable Mary had been most of last winter.

"And remember how Steve really liked Mary and wanted to go out with her, and she wouldn't because of Greg." Laurie K. continued, walking over and sitting down on Becky's dressing table stool. "And Mary was always worried that he was dating somebody else. It's not the greatest way in the world to have a boyfriend," Laurie K. concluded.

"But Tom and I could have made it work."

"I don't know . . ."

"But he really likes me—liked me."

"I shouldn't say this," Laurie K. started, "but it might be better—breaking up."

Becky got up from the bed and walked over to her dresser. Distractedly, she began to rearrange the photos and mementos on its top. There, in a small silver frame, was a copy of the black and white photograph of Tom and Maxwell playing Frisbee. Tom had given it to her right after she helped him paint his room.

"I don't know what to do," Becky said, and for the first time since they had started talking, she felt a lump rise in her throat.

"Should I see him again?" she asked, her back to Laurie K. "It's a week before he has to leave."

"Not for a few days," Laurie K. said. "I know it's hard to accept, but it sounds like it's over." Laurie K. paused. "Give yourself some time. Then, if you want to see him, do. But be careful."

Becky pulled open the top drawer of her dresser. She picked up the picture of Tom and Maxwell. Could she ever get over the fact that it was finished between her and Tom? Was there another boy anywhere in the world like him? She slipped the photograph, face down, under a pile of scarves. Putting her hands on the drawer pulls, she hesitated before slowly closing the drawer.

When she finally turned around there were tears glistening in her eyes. Laurie K. came over and hugged her.

"C'mon," she said, "let's go out and get a Coke."

"No," Becky said, "I think I'll just stay here."

"You want to stay over at my house tonight?"

"I don't think so."

Becky walked Laurie K. to the front door. Laurie K. paused on the stoop. "If you need me, just call."

"Thank you," Becky said. "I will."

Laurie K. smiled and gave Becky a thumbs-up signal.

Becky got into bed and hunched herself under

the covers. She thought about what Laurie K. had said. It was difficult to carry on a long-distance romance. It would be especially difficult with Tom back at school and back into the life he led in Massachusetts.

Suddenly, Becky was exhausted. She turned out her bedside lamp and burrowed deeper under the covers. She would put it all out of her mind and concentrate on getting to sleep.

## 12

**B**ecky slept late the next morning. When she woke up, she didn't have the energy to get out of bed. Leaning her back against the headboard, looking at the pale green walls of her room, she tried not to think about Tom. She admitted, for the first time to herself, that it was truly over between them.

There was a tap on her door. "Can I come in," Todd said from behind the closed door.

"I guess."

He came into the room and sat down in the chair next to Becky's bed.

"You O.K?"

"I guess," Becky said.

Todd was silent for a moment. He tilted back in the chair and rocked slowly backward and forward.

"I'm sorry," he said.

"Mom told you?"

"Yeah." He rocked the chair back down to the floor and leaned toward her. "You want to talk about it?"

"Not really."

"Hey," he said, standing up and sounding incredibly hearty, "you want some breakfast?"

"I don't think so," Becky replied. "But thanks."

"Sure?"

Becky shrugged.

"Well, O.K.," he said. "See you." He walked out of the room but forgot to close the door.

Becky was about to yell at him to close the door and then decided it didn't really matter.

Todd was back almost instantly. He was carrying a large tray heaped with breakfast. He looked sheepish as he walked carefully into the room with the overloaded tray. "I know you said you weren't hungry but . . ."

Becky was pleased. Todd must have had everything ready before he came in to say good morning. At the sight of all the food, she realized she was famished.

Becky scooted her legs up under her and smoothed down the covers. Todd placed the tray in front of her.

"It's beautiful," Becky said. "I guess I am hungry after all. Thank you." She glanced up at Todd, who was smiling in kind of an embarrassed way.

"You're welcome . . ." he paused. "Hey . . . you feel like doing something today? Go to the pool? Or I could teach you my new video game—"

"I have to work," Becky said, "Thanks anyway. It's nice of you to offer."

Todd stood up. "Let me know when you're finished and I'll come and get the tray."

"It's a wonderful breakfast," Becky said. "Thanks again."

She watched Todd as he walked to the door and carefully closed it behind him. What a great little . . . no, she thought, she ought to stop calling him that. What a great brother.

As Becky dressed, she tried not to think about Tom. It was almost an impossible task. She decided she just couldn't just sit around the house, so she went to the library early.

Mrs. Francis suggested that Becky put together a back-to-school display in the Children's Department. It was the first time that Becky had been asked to do a display by herself and she was pleased by the responsibility.

She decided that reference books and information were a good topic for the start of school, so she gathered copies of all the dictionaries and encyclopedic books for kids that she could find and arranged them on top of the low cabinet where they always set up the displays.

Mrs. Francis complimented her on her choice of a theme and on the way she had arranged the books. Next, there was a whole bin of returned books that needed to be reshelved so Becky loaded them onto a rolling cart and began to distribute them in their proper sections. The work was a bit monotonous but Becky really didn't mind doing the shelving. It was the perfect way to get to know more titles and more sections so she took her time and carefully rearranged the books.

She was in the Reference section and was just about finished when a little girl came up to her.

"I need a book on dogs," the girl said. "My Dad just got me a puppy."

"What kind of puppy?" Becky asked as she walked toward the pet section.

"An Irish setter."

Becky stopped in front of the dog books. She felt a lump rise in her throat as she pulled *How To Raise and Train Irish Setters* off the shelf.

"Look at him," the little girl exclaimed. She pointed to the picture of the setter on the cover. "That's just what mine looks like."

An unbidden picture flashed across Becky's mind of a copper-haired boy frolicking with an Irish setter.

"This is just the book," the girl said, breaking into Becky's reverie.

Becky felt the lump in her throat rising. "If you'll go up to the check-out desk," she managed to say, "you can take the book home and learn all about . . . Irish setters."

"Thank you," the girl said. She turned and scurried to the desk.

Becky stood by the window, trying to hold back her tears.

"Are you all right?" a voice behind her asked gruffly.

Becky rubbed her hands across her eyes and turned around. She tried to smile at Mr. Jones. "Sure, I'm okay."

Mr. Jones reached out and patted Becky on the shoulder. "There, there," he whispered.

Becky felt the tears starting again. She sniffed and tried to wipe her nose on her hand. Mr. Jones pulled a fresh white handkerchief from his breast pocket and handed it to her. Becky dabbed at her eyes and blew her nose.

Should she talk to Mr. Jones about Tom? Could she? He had helped her with her first real meeting with Tom and he looked so concerned. It all came pouring out of Becky.

"Oh dear," Mr. Jones said gently. "You need a good cup of tea. Stay right here. I'll arrange it with Sylvia—Mrs. Francis—and we'll step out for a few minutes."

Mr. Jones whispered to Mrs. Francis and then gently, but firmly, marched Becky outside the library and down the street to the drugstore. He deposited her in a secluded booth and ordered two cups of tea with lemon.

In the beginning, Becky was shy about being with him, but he was so sympathetic that soon she had poured out her story.

Mr. Jones stirred his cup of tea slowly. "I'm afraid you've come up against an age-old problem," he said. "One that has tormented young lovers since the beginning of time. I don't know that anyone has ever found a solution. There may not even be," he said, looking at Becky carefully, "a solution."

"I don't understand," Becky said.

"It's hard for us to comprehend, Becky," Mr. Jones said, "that someone like Mrs. Stearns actually knows when and where her forebears arrived in the United States. Those people are as alive to her, and as important, as her living relatives. Boston," he said, "of all the cities in America, is probably more concerned with caste and with history than any other city."

He squeezed the last drop of lemon in his tea. "Social discrimination plays a large part in Boston life."

Is that really what she was facing? Were she and Tom from such different worlds? Was the gap between them so large that they could never find a bridge across it?

"It's too bad you had to face this at such a young age," Mr. Jones said kindly.

"Maybe," Becky started, and found herself frightened by what she was about to say, "maybe it would have been better if I'd never met Tom."

Mr. Jones smiled at her. "I doubt that," he said. "You've had a delightful time with him, haven't you?"

Becky nodded. She guessed they had had a "delightful" time together.

"I daresay it would have been better not to have met Edge," Mr. Jones said. "But don't take Mr. Edgington as an example of everyone from Boston. He simply sounds like a bad lot."

In spite of herself, Becky smiled. Why was it that no one could ever get Edge's name right?

"As for Tom," Mr. Jones continued, "we all need to meet and know people who expose us to new ideas." He reached across the table and patted Becky's hand. "You are still young, my dear," he said, "you can have anything you want, go anywhere you want." For the first time in their conversation, he began to sound like an adult giving advice. "You mustn't let one encounter with people like Mrs. Stearns and Edge sour you on reaching out."

But what did she want? After spending the summer desperately wanting to be a part of Tom's world, Becky realized now, that maybe, just maybe, she should first find out more about Becky Johnson from River Bend, Illinois. She knew, in an unexpected flash of insight, that while Tom's world was different, it was not necessarily better. She had just assumed that it was better all along.

"We should get back," Mr. Jones said, looking at his pocket watch. "I'm afraid I've kept you from your duties long enough." He slid out of the booth and stood up.

"Thank you," Becky said, also standing up. "I don't know . . . I mean . . ."

"It's quite all right, my dear," he said, taking her hand and tucking it snugly into the crook of his arm. "You have had, I'm afraid, a brutal introduction to the ways of the world." He patted her hand. "But I'm sure you're much too strong and intelligent to let it get you down."

They walked back to the library in silence. Becky's head was swirling from their conversation. Did it matter that the Johnsons didn't have a two-hundred-year-old lineage? Did it matter that Becky didn't have a portrait of her great-grandmother that had been painted by a famous painter or that her mother didn't collect antique Chinese vases? Becky had spent so long thinking that those things were important that she was shocked to realize that they really didn't matter very much at all.

When they reached the library, it was just a few minutes before closing and L.W. was waiting anxiously for her.

"How are you?" she asked, a look of worry on her face. "I saw Laurie K. and she told me—"

"I think I'm all right."

"I'll drive you home," L.W. offered. "Do you want to talk about it some more?"

"I'm not sure," Becky answered. "It all seems sort of unreal."

Becky helped close up the library, said goodnight to Mrs. Francis and Miss Stevenson, and got into the car with L.W.

"Let's go to my house," L.W. suggested.

A short while later, they were ensconced in L.W.'s room and Becky had told her the whole story. She couldn't believe it was the third time she had gone over the story but talking about it, going over last night and the events of the summer, helped to put it into perspective, helped to lessen the pain.

L.W. took a sip of her diet cola. "I told you Edge was a jerk," she said. "You musn't let what he said bother you." She dismissed him entirely from their lives with a wave of her hand.

"Tom's an incredible guy," L.W. said, "and I think that his influence on you has been very good. But . . ."

"But what?"

L.W. bit at the skin on her thumb. "But you didn't make all these changes in yourself *for* yourself. You made most of them because you thought they would please Tom."

"But I wanted to change."

"I know you did," L.W. said. "We all do that when we meet somebody we like. It's just natural to become interested in the things that the other person is interested in." She paused and gave Becky a significant look. "For instance, I may take up jogging in the very near future."

"Really?"

L.W. nodded. "But that is another story." She shifted her position on the couch. "I like the way you've been wearing your hair," she said, "and

184

you look good in loafers. But are they the real Becky Johnson?"

Becky was suddenly weary. "Who is the real Becky Johnson?" she asked.

A look of annoyance crossed L.W.'s face. "Don't you dare say that! Becky Johnson is intelligent, she's fun to be around, she's pretty, she's an expert librarian, she's . . ."

Becky blushed at her friend's praise.

"Listen, you nut," L.W. said. "Don't you realize you must have had something going for you or a guy like Tom would have never been interested in the first place? Did you ever think about that?" L.W. demanded. "And he certainly wouldn't have spent the summer hanging around if he hadn't seen an awful lot that he liked."

"Do you really think so?"

"Of course," L.W. said.

"I never thought of it like that. Edge said . . ."

"Forget Edge."

"But . . ."

"No," L.W. said, "Tom obviously saw all your good traits and that's what he liked about you."

"But I made such a fool of myself," Becky said. "With all that opera and culture. All that stuff."

"No you didn't," L.W. corrected Becky. "You never know when there might be a question on the SAT test—or somewhere else—about Beethoven and all the rest!"

"But what about Tom's parents and the whole social thing?"

"His mother must be pretty small-minded if she can't see how terrific you are," L.W. said firmly.

Becky smiled at her. L.W. smiled back. "You're great, kiddo," she said in conclusion. "Even if you do read too much."

L.W. drove Becky home and suggested that they go to a movie that night. Becky declined. She needed some time alone to think and sort things out.

After dinner, Becky put her favorite record on her stereo and settled down on her bed. Talking to Laurie K. and Mr. Jones and L.W. had helped her put her relationship with Tom in perspective. It was funny, she mused, to have gotten three different points of view from her three different friends. Laurie K. had talked about the problems of long-distance romances, Mr. Jones about society and L.W. about how terrific Becky was. Putting all three of those together gave Becky the courage to deal with the breakup.

She knew, deep down inside, that if Tom called right that minute and said he had changed his mind, that he was going to stay in River Bend and that he wanted her back, that she would rush out to meet him.

Or would she?

In her heart of hearts she knew that it was over between them, that no matter what happened, they could never recapture the moments that they had shared. Tom was an amazing guy but he was going away, back East to a life that he belonged to and understood. And Becky was staying in River Bend—at least until she finished high school—and that that was where she belonged.

It was a slow afternoon at the library. Becky had settled herself at the main counter to read through a publisher's catalog of new childrens' books. She was deeply absorbed in the forthcoming titles when she looked up and saw Tom standing on the other side of the desk.

"I found these library books at home," he said. He slipped two thick volumes onto the counter top.

Almost absentmindedly, Becky noticed that he must have recently had a haircut. Most of the golden streaks in his dark hair were gone. Otherwise, he looked very much the same as he had on the first day they had met. How long ago that now seemed!

"These are overdue," she said coolly.

"I know."

"You owe forty cents."

Tom dug into his pocket and pulled out the change. Their hands touched as he laid the coins in her palm.

"It was a great summer," he said softly.

Becky's eyes met his before she turned away to drop the coins in the open drawer beside her.

# First Love from Silhouette

## THERE'S NOTHING QUITE AS SPECIAL AS A FIRST LOVE.

### — $1.95 —

- 24 ☐ DREAM LOVER Treadwell
- 26 ☐ A TIME FOR US Ryan
- 27 ☐ A SECRET PLACE Francis
- 29 ☐ FOR THE LOVE OF LORI Ladd
- 30 ☐ A BOY TO DREAM ABOUT Quinn
- 31 ☐ THE FIRST ACT London
- 32 ☐ DARE TO LOVE Bush
- 33 ☐ YOU AND ME Johnson
- 34 ☐ THE PERFECT FIGURE March
- 35 ☐ PEOPLE LIKE US Haynes
- 36 ☐ ONE ON ONE Ketter
- 37 ☐ LOVE NOTE Howell
- 38 ☐ ALL-AMERICAN GIRL Payton
- 39 ☐ BE MY VALENTINE Harper
- 40 ☐ MY LUCKY STAR Cassiday
- 41 ☐ JUST FRIENDS Francis

- 42 ☐ PROMISES TO COME Dellin
- 43 ☐ A KNIGHT TO REMEMBER Martin
- 44 ☐ SOMEONE LIKE JEREMY VAUGHN Alexander
- 45 ☐ A TOUCH OF LOVE Madison
- 46 ☐ SEALED WITH A KISS Davis
- 47 ☐ THREE WEEKS OF LOVE Aks
- 48 ☐ SUMMER ILLUSION Manning
- 49 ☐ ONE OF A KIND Brett
- 50 ☐ STAY, SWEET LOVE Fisher
- 51 ☐ PRAIRIE GIRL Coy
- 52 ☐ A SUMMER TO REMEMBER Robertson
- 53 ☐ LIGHT OF MY LIFE Harper
- 54 ☐ PICTURE PERFECT Enfield
- 55 ☐ LOVE ON THE RUN Graham

- 56 ☐ ROMANCE IN STORE Arthur
- 57 ☐ SOME DAY MY PRINCE Ladd
- 58 ☐ DOUBLE EXPOSURE Hawkins
- 59 ☐ A RAINBOW FOR ALISON Johnson
- 60 ☐ ALABAMA MOON Cole
- 61 ☐ HERE COMES KARY! Dunne
- 62 ☐ SECRET ADMIRER Enfield
- 63 ☐ A NEW BEGINNING Ryan
- 64 ☐ MIX AND MATCH Madison
- 65 ☐ THE MYSTERY KISS Harper
- 66 ☐ UP TO DATE Sommers
- 67 ☐ PUPPY LOVE Harrell
- 68 ☐ CHANGE PARTNERS Wagner
- 69 ☐ ADVICE AND CONSENT Alexander

*First Love from Silhouette*

- 70 ☐ MORE THAN FRIENDS Stuart
- 71 ☐ THAT CERTAIN BOY Malek
- 72 ☐ LOVE AND HONORS Ryan
- 73 ☐ SHORT STOP FOR ROMANCE Harper
- 74 ☐ A PASSING GAME Sommers
- 75 ☐ UNDER THE MISTLETOE Mathews
- 76 ☐ SEND IN THE CLOWNS Youngblood
- 77 ☐ FREE AS A BIRD Wunsch
- 78 ☐ BITTERSWEET SIXTEEN Bush

- 79 ☐ LARGER THAN LIFE Cole
- 80 ☐ ENDLESS SUMMER Bayner
- 81 ☐ THE MOCKINGBIRD Stuart
- 82 ☐ KISS ME, KIT Francis
- 83 ☐ WHERE THE BOYS ARE Malek
- 84 ☐ SUNNY SIDE UP Grimes
- 85 ☐ IN THE LONG RUN Alexander
- 86 ☐ THE BOY NEXT DOOR Youngblood
- 87 ☐ ENTER, LAUGHING Leroe

- 88 ☐ A CHANGE OF HEART McKenna
- 89 ☐ BUNNY HUG Harper
- 90 ☐ SURF'S UP FOR LANEY Caldwell
- 91 ☐ $R_x$ FOR LOVE Graham
- 92 ☐ JUST THE RIGHT AGE Chatterton
- 93 ☐ SOUTH OF THE BORDER Kingsbury
- 94 ☐ LEAD ON LOVE Hart
- 95 ☐ HEAVENS TO BITSY Harrell
- 96 ☐ RESEARCH FOR ROMANCE Phillips

---

**FIRST LOVE, Department FL/4**
**1230 Avenue of the Americas**
**New York, NY 10020**

Please send me the books I have checked above. I am enclosing
$_____ (please add 75¢ to cover postage and handling. NYS and
NYC residents please add appropriate sales tax). Send check
or money order—no cash or C.O.D.'s please. Allow six weeks for
delivery.

NAME _____

ADDRESS _____

CITY _____ STATE/ZIP _____